Sand Dunes

KAY HOLDEN

authorHOUSE®

AuthorHouse™
1663 Liberty Drive
Bloomington, IN 47403
www.authorhouse.com
Phone: 1 (800) 839-8640

Published by AuthorHouse   09/09/2015

ISBN: 978-1-5049-1567-0 (sc)
ISBN: 978-1-5049-1566-3 (e)

Library of Congress Control Number: 2015908908

Print information available on the last page.

Chapter 1

Three a.m. The salty warm breeze was blowing softly across Sandy Lanstrim's face where she sat hidden in the sand dunes. The dunes were a haven, a place she always came to when she was upset or needed to think. The salt air stung her tear stained face. Sandy was taking a good look at her life and so far it had not been good. Until she was eighteen she had everything she could possible want in life a life Destined for great things. Two loving parents. One spring night the beach was crowded with some people drinking unfortunately driving. Sandy's parents were at the wrong place at the wrong time. Some teens hit their car, killing them both instantly. This was the beginning of a big change in her life. There were no siblings or close relatives that she could lean on. So she had to be strong and stand on her own two feet. All through high school she had made good grades and received a scholarship to North Carolina at Chapel Hill. This had been her parents' dream for her to attend their alma mater. This is where they had fallen in love and got married. It was a special place for them. Her parents hadn't been rich but they left her enough money to live on until she finished school and started on her own.

The first year of college she carried a 4.0 GPA average. All she ever did was study with little socializing and a lot of keeping to herself. Her roommate on the other hand was happy with only a passing grade. Then it was party time. Each time Pam would get ready to go out she would ask Sandy to go along and got the same answer each time. "I have to study." Pam finally gave up asking.

Chapter 2

Summer was here and Sandy returned home to Kure Beach, North Carolina where she had grown up. She opened up her parents' home and felt the hurt of losing them all over again. She could not stay here. She thought she did not want to sell the house but someday she might want to live there again. She talked to Mr. Allen, the man she had worked for since she was sixteen. "Sandy, why don't you take a long-term lease and then you would have some security to fall back on."

Sandy thought about that for a long moment. "I think I will do that," she said as she picked up the phonebook looking for realtors. It didn't take long for a movie studio to take out a five year lease. The house was paid so the money she received could be for a rainy day. Sandy put most of the furnishings into storage and had a garage sale for the things she didn't want. She made enough money from the sale that she could work part time and enjoy the beach. The Allen's had a small efficiency apartment and Sandy rented it. She could look out of her window and see the water and hear the eternal surf roaring day and night. And she could always smell the refreshing salt air. This brought back fond memories of the times that she and her parents spent on the beach together.

Over the summer Sandy came out of her shyness and became more outgoing. She emerged like a beautiful butterfly coming out of her cocoon. Before she knew it, it was time to return to school. Arriving on campus everyone was excited to be back. She had never noticed before but now as she walked across campus heads turned to check her out and she liked it. The sun had streaked her hair giving it a copper golden look, making her emerald eyes even more alluring. Entering her dorm room she found Pam already there and unpacked. "Hi," her roommate called jumping up to give her a hug. "What have you done to yourself? The summer has certainly done wonders for you," Pam said laughing.

"Help me with these bags and I will tell you all about it." They each shared their summer fun and settled in to unpacking.

Classes were not as hard as they were the first year. Sandy took time to date and go to parties. She wasn't dating anyone special. She was just having a good time.

Her junior year was when she met George Roman at a frat party. He was the big man on campus and could have anyone he chose. He was very good looking with dark wavy hair and big brown eyes, the kind that when you looked into them you wanted to take him into your arms and cuddle him. He picked Sandy out of the crowded room and made his move. "Don't I know you," he said as he slipped his arm around her waist.

"I'm sorry but you must have me mixed up with someone else. My name is Sandy Langstrim."

"I am George and if I have never met you before it is my loss," he said smiling. Her face felt like she was wearing a warm mask. It was unsettling yet exciting. From that night on they were inseparable. By Spring Break they were in love. The big prom was the buzz of the campus. George and Sandy were the talk of their group. The question was would they get married or would they just live together? Sandy was not that type of girl to sleep around and that was driving George crazy.

Their Prom was great but the heat of a Southern spring heat was unbearable. George took Sandy's hand and led her out to the gardens. The air was warm and the smell of the flowers was intoxicating. Sandy and George were walking along the garden path when suddenly George swept her into his arms and kissed her passionately leaving her gasping for breath. When they came up for air he placed his hands on both sides of her face. "Would you marry me?"

Sandy was wide eyed with tears running down her face. "Yes" was all she could say. George was talking so fast with making plans for their marriage. It took a few minutes for it all to sink in. He meant next week on Spring Break.

"Why the rush, I thought you meant after school and we had jobs," Sandy said.

"Why wait. I can't keep my hands off of you and you won't live with me so let's not put it off," he said looking at her with his youthful his grin. When he looked at her like that she melted. The word no wasn't an option.

Chapter 3

The next week they went to the Justice of the Peace at City Hall. A small group of friends attended. The ceremony took less than five minutes. This was not what she hoped her wedding would be like. George told her that this was only a piece of paper and what was inside was what counted. A big wedding was a waste of money. After the marriage they found a small apartment off the campus. Everything went fine for the first few weeks.

When she came home from classes the apartment was running over with his friends. Day and night someone was there. There was never any time for lovemaking or just a quiet evening to talk. Their food bill was running between two and three hundred every two weeks. Sandy tried to talk to George about the money they were spending but all he would do was laugh and tell her to go to the bank and get some more money. There were so many beer cans and bottles that she started to recycle them. Sometimes she would get back as much as thirty dollars. Every little bit helped, she thought. It was hard for her to understand why George had turned out this way. This was not the man she thought she married. By their senior year the money was just about gone from their student loans. She decided not to tell George about the lease money from the house or her trust fund that she had tucked away. This was to be her fallback money as Mr. Allen had suggested. She was glad that she had listened to him.

"George, we are almost out of money. We have enough for this month and that's it. We need to get part time jobs to make ends meet until graduation."

"I tell you what. Why don't you drop out of school and work? When I graduate and find a good paying job you can finish. If I have to work my grade point would drop and I would not graduate with honors. That would keep me from starting at the top entry level of some of the companies I am looking at."

He walked over to Sandy and put his arms around her and gently kissed her lips, something he hadn't done for a while.

Sandy was tired of fighting about money so she agreed. She found work as a waitress at a local diner. The people were nice and they liked her. The money was good with the tips. She had to work split shift so she didn't see much of George. Graduation was in only two days and many things would change.

Chapter 4

Graduation came and went. George was in no hurry to look for work. His excuse was that he was tired and was going to take his time looking for work. He wasn't going to take the first thing that came along.

Several months after school was out Sandy decided to go home to check on George. That morning he was complaining that he was sick and couldn't look for work. Sandy had never gone home between shifts before. As she entered the apartment she could hear moaning coming from the bedroom. He really must be sick she thought as she opened the door. She stopped and stared at the bed, there was George lying on his back with some blonde headed girl on top of him riding like the wind. At first they were so involved with each other they didn't see her standing there. Sandy didn't say a word, she went to the closet and threw her things in the suitcase and started to walk out. George and the girl never moved. George said, "I suppose that it wouldn't do any good to say I'm sorry." Sandy just looked at him and walked out.

After the divorce she heard that he was working for a big corporation and making big bucks. She knew he had only used her and she was better off without him. She lost all interest in finishing school. She took several different jobs trying to find herself so to speak. She felt as though her life had no meaning. These days she had never felt so alone. It had been a year now and it was time to get back to her roots. She moved back to Kure Beach. Here is where she felt she belonged. She always loved the beach. This was a place to relax and get her life back on track. It was off season, so it wasn't hard to find an apartment on the water. After everything was in its place it was time to find a job. Sandy went to work for Dean Smith Travel Agency. She worked very hard to learn everything she could about the business. She had a friendly way about her making all the customers feel special. They were so pleased with the treatment they had received that they told their friends and the workload increased by fifty percent.

Chapter 5

As Sandy worked she could feel Dean watching her; she wasn't sure if it was work related or personal. Dean and Sandy had to work late one night, neither had eaten so Dean asked her to dinner. This was the beginning of their romance. They spent all their time together at home and work. They were at Dean's apartment sitting on the couch in front of the roaring fire having wine. Dean put his arm around her shoulder and said, "Sandy, why don't you move in with me? You are here more than at your place."

Sandy thought about it long and hard but the thought of giving up her place was unbearable. Dean had never said the words that would have made the difference. She needed to hear I love you. He had never so much as hinted at these words. "I think that it is best to keep things like they are for now but thanks for asking."

Dean leaned over and lightly gave her a peck on the lips and got up for more wine. It sort of hurt her feelings that he didn't try a little harder to convince her. In her heart she knew she had made the right decision.

Chapter 6

Business had increased even more and it was time to hire another person. Wendy Ann Smutty was hired. She was not what Sandy would have chosen but she wasn't the boss. Wendy was twenty-one, long brown hair, brown eyes with the longest eyelashes with the question if they were real or fake. When some of the men clients came they sometimes forgot why they were there. Shortly after Wendy joined the group Dean talked about enlarging his business, he told Sandy he had to meet with investors and began having a lot of late business meetings. This was going on for weeks. They were spending less time together out of the office and talked only business in the office. Sandy entered Dean's office and closed the door behind her. "Dean, is there something going on that I should know about, you are not yourself lately?"

"No my love it is just that I have all the pressure on me. I am trying to build this business for us. If I have neglected you I will make it up to you soon I promise."

Friday was here and the atmosphere was very secretive. Today Wendy kept looking at Sandy and smiling. Wendy was in and out of Dean's office all day long and each time she came out she had a sheepish grin. Late in the afternoon the florist delivered two dozen red long stem roses to Sandy. She was very surprised, no one had ever sent her flowers before. When she opened the card it said will you have dinner with me tonight, love Dean. Sandy could feel the tears run down her face as she went to Dean's office and gave him a big hug. Dean took her to the finest restaurant in town. They had the finest wine and food money could buy. Sandy thought this was going to be the night Dean asked her to marry him. He had never used the word love before and had never been this extravagant. This had to be what he had in mind. After dinner while sipping their brandy, Dean reached over and took her hand and stroked it lovingly. "Sandy, I have something to tell you and I want you to know this is very hard for me. I have found someone else. I feel like a heel for not telling you sooner but I wasn't sure it would last. We have had good times together and now it's time to move on with our lives and take new directions."

Sandy just looked at him not believing what she heard. Dean just kept talking as though this was a business meeting. These were the facts, no big deal. "You know the meetings I have been having at night, well I am closing the agency and moving to Las Vegas. I have big money backing me and the money is just there waiting to be taken."

"Who is she?" Sandy asked.

"It is Wendy. We didn't plan for this to happen but it did."

Sandy thought Wendy didn't plan any of this. In a pig's-eye! She wasn't going to give him the satisfaction of seeing her cry. "Could you take me home now?"

"Yes, sure I can." Dean looked for the waiter to pay the check. Sandy didn't wait for him. She walked outside to the car. Dean arrived at her side and opened the door for her neither saying a word.

The tension in the car was so thick you could cut it with a knife on the ride home. Sandy broke the silence and asked "How long before you close the agency?"

"In four weeks that will give us enough time to clear out all the business. It means that we are all going to have to work very hard to get everything done on time. What makes him think I will show up to work tomorrow, she thought. Getting out of the car Dean caught her hand and said, "I hope that I haven't hurt you."

"All I can say is that I hope you get everything in life you deserve and I wish you and Wendy well," she said closing the door in his face.

Chapter 7

Inside the apartment the tears began to flow. How could I be so stupid? This can't be happening to me again. She changed her clothes and headed for the beach. The Dunes always helped her to put things into perspective. Deep in thought and crying she didn't hear the stranger come up behind her. "Hello, are you okay?" Quint asked.

Sandy jumped as she wiped the tears from her face. "I am fine," she said as she turned to look at the person who dared to intrude on her space. As she looked up there stood this handsome man six feet or more, great tan which shown in the bright moon light. "May I sit down?" Not waiting for an answer, he was sitting next to her. She was looking into the clearest blue eyes she had ever seen. "Isn't it a little late to be up in the dunes by yourself?" Quint asked.

"Again I am just fine. I always come here so could you please leave," Sandy ordered.

"When you are upset it helps to talk to someone who is not close to the problem. I am willing to listen."

Sandy was stunned that a stranger would be interested in someone else's problem. He had such a caring voice and tenderness in his face. He held out his hand. "My name is Quint."

Sandy took his hand. "Mine is Sandy." Before she knew it she was telling him about her evening with Dean and what a fool she had been for not seeing it coming.

"The only fool is Dean for letting someone like you get away."

Sandy blushed. "Quint, what are you doing out this late?" she asked.

"You know, woman trouble." They both laughed. Sandy didn't realize how good it felt to talk to someone. Quint got quiet and looked into her jade green eyes. He ever so gently took her into his arms and placed soft kisses on her lips then her eye lids then back to her lips. Sandy was shocked at first but responded to his kiss. They came up for air and this time he held her a little tighter and kissed her more passionately. Sandy responded to his demanding kiss. She felt at this point he was a life line. She needed to feel that someone wanted her and Quint was that person for the moment. It had been a long time since Quint had held anyone in his arms and he didn't want to let her go. She was warm and alive. Slowly he rubbed her nipples through her halter top. Sandy responded to his every touch. He began to remove her top with no resistance. He placed soft kisses along her neck and down to her firm breasts. He took her nipples in his mouth and began to suck so very gentle until they were very hard. The kisses were moved down her abdomen then to her inner thighs. Sandy had never felt like this with anyone before. The feelings were frightening but at the same time felt so good. Quint unsnapped her shorts and gently removed them leaving her naked on the beach towel she had been sitting on. He quickly stood and removed his own clothes. As he did so Sandy watched with wonderment. He had the most beautiful body she had ever seen. Strong shoulders, flat stomach and his manhood was quite large. Quint lowered his body over her and began where he had left off. His kisses were gentle at first but became more demanding. Sandy met his every demand and couldn't believe she was able to give herself to a perfect stranger but there was no turning back now. Quint sliding his hand between her thighs inserted one finger into her folds of passion. He found her warm and wet as he stroked her. She arched her body toward him wanting more. Sandy felt if he didn't enter her now she would explode. Sensing her need he entered her very slow with even slower strokes. At first it was like a tease, then the strokes began to increase. He stopped.

"Am I hurting you?"

Sandy smiled and said, "No."

Quint started again this time not so gentle.

Sandy met each stroke with the same thrust, her whole body was shaking. Their passion spent, Quint took her in his arms a long time not wanting to let her go, neither saying a word. The guilt came over him about Shelby and he had to leave. He kissed her one last time and got dressed.

"I hate to leave you here. Can I take you home?"

"I am just fine but thanks for asking."

One last kiss and he turned and walked down the beach. They each took what they needed from each for the moment. There was an unspoken word between them that they would not see each again. As Quint walked down the beach the realization set in that they had not used protection. She called after him but he just kept walking. She ran to the water and washed herself as best as she could. During their passion she had not given any thought to AIDS or social diseases. This never crossed her mind. She only wanted to be held and made to feel special. Quint had shown her what it was really like to have someone to make you feel special. She had never experienced anything like their lovemaking before.

Chapter 8

After arriving home she showered for a long time and used a douche trying to wash any remains of their passion. All she could think about was the song Reba sang, "John." After her shower she went to bed. In sleep all she dreamed about was Quint. She awoke late still in a fog asking herself if last night was a dream or did it really happen. Fully awake drinking her coffee she knew it was no dream. The first thing Sandy did was call the doctor's office and make an appointment to have an exam and AIDS test. It would be three weeks before she could be seen. She would have to get on with her life until then. The next call was to Dean. Wendy answered the phone.

"Where are you?" she demanded.

"I am not coming into work today," Sandy said.

"What do you mean, we have a lot of tickets to write today and if you don't come in Dean and I will have to work late," Wendy whined.

"Sorry, I am not coming in; have fun," Sandy said with a little laugh.

"Dean is really going to be mad," Wendy snapped.

"So what is he going to do, fire me," and she hung up the phone.

After taking another shower to clear her head she had to admit to herself that she wanted to hurt Dean but may have only hurt herself. It was hard for her to believe she let something like this happen with a stranger.

The next day Sandy went to work, she didn't want to but she had clients to take care of, it wasn't their fault she got dumped. She entered the office with a smile on her face and acted like she didn't have a care in the world. She was determined not to let them know how much she was hurting inside. The days flew by fast. Sandy took care of her clients and sent them on great vacations.

Wendy did everything she could to rub it in that she had Dean. She would go into his office and close the door behind her and with blinds on the window. When she would come out she made a point to straighten her clothes and repair her lipstick all the time looking at Sandy with a fake smile on her face. In three days Dean would be out of her life for good. Now that she had time to think about it she was glad. If he had not broken off with her she might never have known what it was like to have been made love to the way Quint had shown her. Dean and George only knew one way, what pleased them. They forgot all about her needs. Not knowing any better she accepted the fact that this was the way lovemaking was. Dean was so routine you knew what was coming every time, never any change.

Sandy had to find a new job. She had offers from several big agencies in town. She wanted to take some time to pick the best one for her. The offer from Winnie Lewis was the one that suited her the best. The office was warm and friendly. Winnie made her feel like family. Before she took the job she was going to take a vacation. While working for Dean there was never any time it was work, work, and work. She booked a cruise to Freeport for three days. With her discount it was very cheap and she needed to get away before starting over.

Chapter 9

Quint Jordan was forty-one years old, a very successful attorney. He had married his college sweetheart upon graduation. They had it all. After two years with the firm Wise, Wise and Wise he made full partner. The practice was growing by leaps and bounds. His wife Shelby was a stay at home wife which she loved. She made each evening as special as possible. He never knew what he would find when he arrived home. On one occasion he found her wrapped in a big red bow. That was a night to remember. They had been married two years and no signs of a baby. Shelby made appointment with the specialist in fertility problems. At first it was take the temperature every day. Then when that didn't work the sperm count was next. Quint felt embarrassed having to put his sperm in the cup and hand it to the nurse. The nurse looked at him and smiled. He knew she was having dirty thoughts the way she smiled at him. He was never so glad to get out of an office in his life. Quint loved Shelby so much he would do anything for her and today that love had been proven. Shelby was obsessive with having a baby. In fact, that was all she thought about. They had talked about adopting a baby but Shelby would not hear of it, she wanted her own baby or nothing. She took fertility pills with no luck. After everything else failed in-vitro fertilization was the last try. They had been married twelve years and they both agreed if this didn't work that they would stop trying. Today was the day Shelby went for her checkup. Quint couldn't get out of his court date he had tried to get his case postponed but no luck. Shelby entered Dr. Goldberg's office.

"Well how do you feel today?" he asked in a warm caring voice.

"Fine," Shelby replied. "I feel like today is the day," she said with a happy smile.

"Well get undressed and I will be back in to examine you," he said as he left the room. After he examined her he told her to get dressed and come into his office. Shelby dressed quickly and entered his office.

"Shelby, have a seat. I want to go over the test results with you," he said as he motioned to the seat in front of his desk.

"Well, I am all ears," she said with a big grin on her face until she looked at the doctor's face.

"Shelby, we have tried everything known to man to get you to conceive a child but nothing has worked. I am so sorry but there is nothing we can do. Have you thought about adopting? I know some young girls that are looking for good homes for their babies."

"You don't understand I want my own," she said and with that statement she picked up her purse and ran out of his office. At home Shelby threw herself across her bed and cried. She just couldn't feel like a failure anymore. Feeling she had denied Quint a baby he deserved, how could she face him? Still crying she entered the bathroom and took down a full bottle of sleeping pill's she filled a glass with water and began to take the pills one by one. Quint came home as soon as court was over hoping to find a very happy wife. When he came into the house he called out to her but no answer. He checked the lower rooms then went upstairs to their bed room. As he opened the door he gasped as he saw Shelby lying on the floor. Running to her he bent down to try and wake her shaking and calling her name no response. He checked for breathing and pulse; both were weak. He picked up the phone and called 911 and pleaded for help. Shelby was taken to the emergency room where Quint gave the E.R. doctor the empty pill bottle he had found at her side.

Chapter 10

Quint prayed she would be all right. The doctors pumped her stomach and tried to reverse the effects of the drug. Shelby stopped breathing and had to be placed on life support; she had not come out of the pill induced coma.

"The next forty eight hours will tell if we got her in time. She has been transferred to the intensive care unit where she can be monitored very closely. You can see her once they have her settled," the E.R. doctor told Quint.

Quint entered the unit and sat next to Shelby's bed looking at her she was so pale. Holding her hand he kept blaming himself for not going to the doctor's office with her. This can't be happening, what could he have told her that was so bad?

"Shelby, you are all I ever needed. A baby would have been nice but you are more important to me. Please don't leave me, I can't go on without you," he said, the tears streaming down his face. Quint felt a hand on his shoulder and turned to see his Sister Betty standing there. Standing he put his arms around her and held her tight.

"Quint, come on let me take you home, the nurses have instructions to call if there is any change."

Quint didn't resist and followed Betty out. At home Betty explained to Quint what happened in Dr. Goldberg's office. She had seen him in the hall outside the unit and told him what had happened. He explained what had gone on and how she had ran out of his office.

"Try and get some rest. I will stay until we find out something," Betty said.

"I don't think I will go into our bedroom. I will lay on the couch. Promise me you will wake me if the hospital calls."

"You know I will. Now rest. You are going to need it." Betty kissed him lightly on the forehead.

After a week the doctors did one more brain wave test called an EEG, and the results were the same as the night Shelby came into the hospital a flat line no brain activity at all. Dr. Gomez asked to take her off life support. He explained to Quint that taking her off life support didn't mean she couldn't live, they would have to see what happened when they took her off the respirator. This was a very hard decision to make but he knew she would not want to be kept alive like this. Shelby was off the machines, her blood pressure held and she was breathing on her own. She had a strong heart considering the effects of the drugs. Doctors decided to feed her through a tube in her nose that went into her stomach. Dr. Gomez took Quint into his office and closed the door.

"Have a seat, Quint, I need to talk to you about Shelby's condition. It is not cost effective to keep

Shelby here at the hospital. I have checked into several private care facilities that are very good. I would like for you to check them out and pick one out by the end of the week then we start the paperwork to transfer her."

"How do I know which is best for Shelby?" Quint asked with tears in his eyes. At this point Quint broke down and cried for the first time realizing his life with Shelby had all but ended. Quint chose a place near their home. It was close to the home and was very clean. The patients were well kept and groomed. Most patients had smiles on their faces and the staff treated the patients with loving care. After Shelby's transfer the weeks turned into months, months into years.

Chapter 11

The strain was taking its toll on Quint. He wasn't able to sleep and not eating properly. Every time the phone rang he was afraid the home was calling him with bad news. He has an appointment with Dr. Gomez late this afternoon.

"Come in," Dr. Gomez said holding out his hand to shake Quint's. "I am sorry I don't have good news for you. Shelby's condition is declining every day. I feel it will only be a matter of hours now before she is gone. Her vital signs are dropping and respirations are shallow. "Thank you for coming in and if there is anything I can do for you please call me."

Quint shook hands with Dr. Gomez and went to Shelby's room. Sitting at her bedside in the dark holding her hand telling her how much he loved her and how he was going to miss her. Dr. Gomez entered the room and placed his hand on Quint's shoulder.

"She's gone." Quint collapsed into the chair and began to cry.

The arrangement had to be made for the funeral. Quint asked his sister Betty to help him, he just couldn't do it by himself. He was in a daze most of the time and didn't know what to do next. He had plenty of time before her death to make all the preparations but then he would have had to admit that she was dying. Home alone he found himself yelling, "Why, why did you do this to us. I loved you."

Awakening the next morning his head was pounding from crying so much he took an aspirin while waiting on Betty. He was on his fourth cup of coffee when she arrived.

"How was your night?" She looked at his puffy face and knew it had been a rough one. "Well big brother it's time to go and get it over with. The longer we wait the harder it will be."

At the funeral home they had to look at caskets, which was the hardest part for him.

"Betty, I just can't do this, could you pick out something?"

Betty took charge, from ordering the flowers for the casket to picking out what Shelby was to wear down to the last detail.

Taking Quint home, she made him pack a bag. She was not going to let him stay alone again tonight. Quint was very glad he wasn't going to stay in the house, every time he walked into their bedroom he still saw her on the floor.

Chapter 12

Two days before her cruise she kept her appointment with Dr. Ray, who had been her doctor since high school. As she entered the doctor's office she was shown to the exam room this was the first time she didn't have to wait and today she wished she did.

"Well Sandy what's going on with you?" asked Dr. Ray.

"I need an AIDS test." Sandy would not look at Dr. Ray in the eye.

"That won't be a problem but is there a specific reason for this request?"

"I did something very stupid. I had unprotected sex with a stranger."

"How long ago?" he asked.

"Three weeks ago."

"Well looking at your chart you are on birth control pills so we don't have to worry about pregnancy."

"No, I had to stop them because of the side effects. It has been six months since I have taken anything."

"When is your next period due?"

"Next week on the twenty-eighth. Why?"

"You are a fertile young woman, it's not impossible for you to become pregnant."

"I haven't given that much thought, I am more concerned about AIDS," Sandy said.

"Well we will get blood for both just to be on the safe side."

"How long will it take to get the results back? I want to go on a cruise in two days." Sandy wanted the results as soon as the blood was drawn but she knew this was impossible. Dr. Ray explained that all his labs had to be sent out and it would take four weeks to get the AIDS test results back. The pregnancy test would be back in a week.

"Gina will draw your blood and I will call you when I get the results back. Have a good trip and don't worry."

Sandy had gone to school with Gina and felt embarrassed for her to know what the tests were for but she had no choice but to let her draw the blood.

"Sandy, have a seat while I get everything ready."

Sandy was shaking a little. Gina put Sandy at ease while talking about old classmates. When Gina was finished drawing the blood she put a cartoon Band-Aid on her arm and told her she was a good patient. They both laughed saying good-bye. Sandy couldn't wait to get out of the office.

Chapter 13

She realized she had not eaten and was getting hungry. The café was across from her new job at Lewis Travels. She might as well try it since she would most likely eat here a lot. Sandy entered the café, it was crowded and she had to stand in line for a table. Looking around the tables it had a small vase of flowers on each table. The wall had pictures of sports and movie personalities which all had been autographed. The pleasant aroma of fresh bread and soup or stew made her even hungrier. The waitress asked several men sitting alone if they would mind sharing their table, each said no. The waitress came and seated the men in front of her and returned for Sandy. You can share a table or wait for about ten minutes. Sandy looked around and decided to share a table. The waitress showed her to the table where the men were reading the newspaper. Sandy sat down and thanked the man for sharing his table. The man never lowered the paper.

"You are welcome," he replied from behind his paper. The waitress was there to take their order.

"I will have a cup of soup and a tuna sandwich with tea to drink."

"That sounds good, I'll have the same," said the voice from behind the paper.

The man finally lowered the paper and looked at Sandy.

"Hello my name is Bill Lewis, sorry about the paper but lunch time is the only time I have a chance to read it..."

"My name is Sandy Langstrim, if you own the travel agency across the street I am your newest employee."

"Oh yes, my wife told me she had hired someone to help us run the office. Welcome aboard, I hear you have a lot of experience. Hopefully you can take some of the workload off my wife and me so we can take advantage of some of our travel plans. It will also be nice to have a pretty face around."

Thank you, I am looking forward to working for you."

As they sat and ate their lunch she felt as though she was being watched. Looking around she couldn't see anyone so she just brushed the feeling off. After finishing her lunch she excused herself.

"I will see you bright and early on Monday." She shook Mr. Lewis's hand and left.

Chapter 14

Aboard the *Princess Ann* Sandy was caught in the excitement of the crowds around her all the laughing and the fun everyone was having. She found her cabin and opened the door. It was a very tiny room. Oh well she thought the price was right and she didn't plan to spend much time in the cabin. She unpacked her things and put her swimsuit on and headed to the pool. Finding an empty lounge chair she settled in with her book. Sandy looked up to find a young woman staring at her, she smiled at her and returned to reading her book.

"Hi, my name is Nancy Winters, are you on this cruise alone?"

"Yes my name is Sandy."

"Good," Nancy said. "I have never done anything like this before and it is a little scary".

"Neither have I maybe we can hang out together," said Sandy.

"Great, I was hoping you would feel that way."

"It's getting late, do you want to meet for dinner?" Nancy asked.

"Sounds good, but don't they assign tables. If we are not at the same table we could meet in the lounge at nine thirty," Sandy said.

Back in her cabin things didn't seem so bad. Sandy thought she might even have a good time. As luck would have it she and Nancy were seated at the same table. The other people at the table were a couple on their honeymoon, a retired couple from Jonestown, Pennsylvania and three single men. Nancy touched Sandy's leg under the table and said in a low voice, "Not bad pickings," then laughed.

After dinner James Watson, Charles and Steve West asked the girls to join them for drinks in the lounge. Sandy and Nancy both agreed. Sandy didn't know when the last time she had this much fun. Before returning to her cabin at four a.m. they all agreed to meet for brunch.

Chapter 15

Nine thirty she dragged herself out of bed and showered with cool water to wake up and hoping her head would stop hurting. If the shower didn't work then the aspirin might. Sandy didn't like taking pills of any kind they were always the last resort. Up on deck everyone was standing around waiting on her. The food was laid out on a long table with all sorts of decoration and anything you could possibly want to eat. Everyone piled their plates high with food except Sandy. Coffee and juice was about all she could handle. Her stomach was a little upset probably too much brandy last night.

When the ship docked at Freeport the five of them decided to see the sights together onshore, the men tolerated the women shopping but were glad when they were finished. The men chose the next place they would venture. The place was called Casino Royale when you walked in it took your breath away it was so beautiful. Rich thick red carpet that when you stepped on it felt like walking on clouds. Palm trees everywhere, fresh flowers with a tropical themed wall with mirrors trimmed in gold. Walls that could slide open when weather permitted to let the sun and fresh air flow through the huge room. Each had their own idea as to what they wanted to play so each went in different direction. Sandy had never gambled before but it looked like fun. She got her tokens for the machines and started putting the tokens in. The first three she got nothing. In went three more, this time she hit the jackpot for 1000 dollars. She just stood there looking in disbelief. The casino paid her in cash. Looking around she decided to play roulette. It took her a few tries to learn to play but it was fun. She didn't win at this game but she didn't lose either. Looking at her watch the time had gotten away from her, it was time to meet the others. The others were on their second drink when she joined them. They teased her that she was late again. They began discussing how much they each had won or lost. Sandy had won the most so she got to pay for the drinks. Returning to the ship Sandy was very tired and begged off from going to the pool.

"I really need a nap before dinner," she said. Entering her cabin she collapsed on her bed and fell sound to sleep. She awoke to a loud knock on her door. "What is it?" Sandy called out trying to get her eyes open.

"It's Nancy." Sandy let her in.

"What's going on? It's almost eight o'clock," said Nancy.

Now wide awake Sandy hurried to get ready for dinner. At eight thirty the girls arrived at their dining table where Charles, Steve and James were waiting on them. Sandy and Nancy were met with low whistles. Their dresses were low cut and short. Dinner was very pleasant, everyone shared how their day went. The girls were invited to go dancing after dinner which they were pleased to accept. Around one a.m. Sandy suddenly became very tired and sick to her stomach. Ate too much she thought. She asked to be excused. Steve escorted her back to her cabin.

"Are you going to be all right? Do you want me to get the ship's doctor?"

"No I will be fine thank you for a lovely evening." Steve kissed her lightly on the cheek and returned to the others. She barely got out of her clothes before she was asleep. The next morning at 10 a.m. Nancy showed up at her door with coffee, juice and a roll. Sandy was very thankful for this morning she was very hungry. Eating the roll with the juice and finishing the coffee she suddenly felt sick and heaved all that she had eaten. Nancy called out to Sandy, "Are you okay?"

"Yes it must be all the rich food we have been eating. I am not used to this kind of food." They decided to stay on the ship today and just lay around the pool and take in the sun.

The cruise had come to an end and they were docking at the port. The group of five had become friends for a short time it hard to say good-by but it was a time they would always remember. Nancy and Sandy decided to keep in touch, they only lived four hours apart by car.

Chapter 16

Monday morning Sandy started her new job. When she entered her office there was a beautiful vase of fresh cut flowers on her desk. The card said welcome from the staff. The atmosphere was warm and friendly she was glad she had chosen this agency to work for. Sandy worked hard and steady trying to get their system down pat. Each office had their own way of doing things and this office was no different. By Friday everything was under control she had even shown the staff some short cuts she had learned. The weekend was here and she was ready for a rest.

Saturday was a kickback day just the usual things to do. Shopping for food was first on the list she was out of just about everything. She usually shopped at the small market near her house but today she chose to go across town to the big market. Going up and down the aisles everything looked good, things she would normally pass up went into her basket. While at the produce counter she felt the hair on the back of her neck stand up. She felt someone was watching her. Looking around she couldn't see anyone. Finishing her shopping she headed home. Putting her groceries away a sudden wave of nausea hit her it passed just as quickly. Time for a nap she thought. Awakened to darkness outside she couldn't believe she had slept so long. The weather was warm and a long walk on the beach sounded good. The water was calm and warm with the salt spray splashing on her legs. The beach was filled with young couples arm and arm the look of love on their faces. Times like this she wished she had a true love but she will just have to wait. I can't always have bad luck with men she thought.

Chapter 17

Arriving home the light on the answering machine was blinking. It was Gina, the nurse from Dr. Ray's office.

"Dr. Ray needs to see you first thing in the morning, no appointment needed."

The machine went silent. For a short time Sandy had put the AIDS test out of her mind. Thinking that if he was having her come in, the test must be positive. There was no chance for food or sleep this night. As soon as the office opened she was there. Dr. Ray took her back to his office and had her to take a seat.

She was so scared she was shaking and could not look at him.

"Sandy, part of the test has come back, the pregnancy test is positive." She looked up at him in disbelief and shook her head no.

"This can't be happening to me," she cried.

"Yes it can, what do you want to do about the baby?"

Sandy looked at Dr. Ray not understanding what he was talking about. He realized and explained you can keep the baby, put it up for adoption or have an abortion.

"Do I have to make a choice now?" she asked in a quiet voice.

"Of course not take your time," he said in a paternal manner.

Sandy remembered about the AIDS test. "How long will it take for the results to get back?"

"Only a few more days. I will call you with the results soon."

She was in a daze when she left the office.

Returning home she called the office and told them that she was not going to be returning to work today. Sitting in front of the TV not hearing the sound or seeing the picture she just stared going over her choices. She knew she couldn't have an abortion or give it away. Realizing at that moment it was her baby and she would keep it. With a big smile on her face she realized where the upset stomach came from and gently rubbed her belly, thinking my baby, all mine. There was a lot to think about and plans to be made. She was going to be a single mom and that didn't sound so bad. Tuesday she called and made an appointment with Dr. Goldberg's office her OB GYN. It would be four weeks before she could be seen. Now she was getting excited.

Work went smooth this week she had not gotten sick to her stomach once. The phone rang at her desk; it was Dr. Ray.

"Sandy, good news the AIDS test was negative, you can relax for now. We will repeat in six months then you can put it behind you.

"Thank you, this means a lot to me."

"I thought it would, is everything else okay?"

"Just great. I am going to keep my baby."

"I am glad you are. Now if there is anything you need just call me."

"Again thank you for everything," she said and hung up the phone.

Chapter 18

Weeks went by and Quint was having a hard time adjusting to the fact Shelby was gone. The only place he went was to work and home. Betty would insist he come over and have dinner at least once a week. He knew she would hound him if he didn't give in he knew she loved him and only cared about his welfare. Tonight at dinner they talked about how he was getting along.

"Quint, it has been three years since you have taken any time off I think you need a vacation," Betty informed him.

"I don't feel like a vacation," he said.

"Well you just think about a trip maybe even a cruise," Betty told him with a determined look on her face.

"I will think about it," he said.

"You know you might as well give in, she isn't going to give up until you take some time off," Bill his brother in law informed him. Quint smiled and agreed with him.

A few days went by and he hadn't spoken to Betty. He heard his intercom come on. "Mr. Jordan, your sister is here to see you."

"Send her in please, Kelly." Betty entered his office with a pixie smile on her face.

"Okay, what are you up to?" he asked.

"Well get ready to choose your cruise. I have some brochures for you to look at."

"I told you I didn't need a vacation," he said.

"Yes you do, you have until Friday at four to make up your mind. I have made an appointment with a travel agency you will keep or I will choose for you." She turned and headed for the door, then turned to look at him one last time, blew him a kiss and winked. Then she closed the door. Quint sat in his chair looking out the window laughing to himself. He knew he had to keep the appointment or she would choose for him.

Chapter 19

Friday was always busy. She had one last appointment before she could go home. Looking at her watch, he was late. I will have time to freshen up she thought going to the ladies room. As she came out she saw a man at her desk. As she walked closer to her desk the man turned and looked at her. She stopped in her tracks and stood looking at him. He was stunned also, not knowing what to do. Quint stood and held out his hand. "I am Quint Jordan."

"I am Sandy Langstrim," she said as she took his hand she felt a warm shock wave run through her body. It was hard for her not to stare at his blue eyes, they were even more clear than she remembered. She regained her composure and took her hand back.

"How can I help you, Mr. Jordan?" Sandy asked.

"Nice to see you again," he said.

Sandy didn't know what to say and just smiled.

"My sister Betty feels that I need a vacation since my wife's recent death." Sandy looked surprised and hurt at the same time, it had never occurred to her he might be married.

"Let me explain but not here, have dinner with me?" he asked. She started to say no but remembered the baby this would be a good chance to find out what kind of man he is. She agreed to meet him at a local restaurant at seven.

"Shall we discuss your travel plans since you are here?" she asked.

"I think they will have to be put on hold for now, please don't tell Betty. She would not leave me alone if she thought I hadn't made plans." He laughed but Sandy didn't laugh.

At seven she entered the restaurant to find him already seated at a table. He stood and waited for her to join him. They had the usual greetings then sat and were quiet for the first few minutes. He offered her wine. She started to accept but remembered the baby.

"No thanks a soft drink will be fine." Quint looked at her noting how she had taken over his soul since that night. He also felt guilty because he had just buried his wife and now he was looking at this woman with great desire.

"Sandy, I owe you an explanation. The night I met you on the beach I felt that my whole world was coming apart at the seams. The doctors had just told me it was just a matter of days before Shelby would be dead. They wanted to use her as an organ donor and she didn't want that. She really died two years ago, only the shell of her body remained. It is still hard to let her go. When I saw you I just needed to talk to someone that didn't know what was going on in my life. I needed to hold someone real and there you were. I want you to know I don't sleep around, I still felt married to Shelby. When you called my name

I wanted to go back but I couldn't. If I had gone back I wouldn't wanted to leave you."

Sandy listened very close looking into his blue eyes.

"I have never done anything like that either but like you I was hurting also. I guess we helped each other out that night." Sandy smiled at him and he agreed.

"We started out as strangers, got the sex out of the way, maybe we can be friends if that's okay... Oh did I tell you that it was incredible sex." Sandy blushed from the top of her head to the tip of her toes.

"I would like to be friends," she said.

"That's a start.

Sandy was on cloud nine until suddenly she was brought back to earth with an upset stomach. Should she tell him about the baby, not yet she thought. I have to get to know this man better than the others I have been involved with. No more mistakes, everything has to go slow. If he wants to be a part of this baby's life that would be okay, if not that's okay too and if I decide to tell him.

Chapter 20

Sunday Quint called and invited Sandy out for ice cream and a walk on the beach. Sandy agreed. He picked her up in his four wheel drive just in case she would rather drive than walk down the beach.

"Hi," he said when she opened the door. His heart was pounding like a schoolboy. Sandy looked like an angel standing there, her red hair flowing, her jade green eyes sparkling. It took his breath away just looking at her.

"Are you ready?"

"Yes," she said as she closed the door.

Sandy was glad he brought his 4 x 4, now they can go to the inlet. This was an isolated part of the beach. As they put down a blanket they were at ease with each other. It felt like they had known each all their lives.

The hours flew by as Quint told Sandy all about Shelby. Sandy in return told about her life. As the sun began to set he asked her if she was ready for ice cream.

"I'll have a double dip, please," she said.

Chapter 21

Monday came all too soon. Sandy had a lot of work to get done this week. Nancy was coming this weekend and she had to make plans for activities for them to do. She was rushing around the office and became a little light headed, the next thing she knew she awoke on the floor. When she opened her eyes everyone was looking down at her. Winnie was placing cold towels to her forehead. Winnie asked if she needed an ambulance. Sandy shook her head no.

"I'll be okay," she said very weakly. At that moment Quint chose to enter the office. He walked back to where everyone was standing and gasped when he looked down and saw her on the floor. He pushed everyone out of the way, bent down and asked, "What happened to you?"

"I just got a little dizzy," she said. Quint gently picked her up and took her into Lewis's office and placed her on the couch.

"Did someone call a doctor?" he barked.

"That's not necessary," she said as she sat up. "I guess I forgot to eat this morning."

Everyone looked relieved.

"Sandy, you go to lunch right now young lady," ordered Winnie and Lewis.

She made her way to the powder room to freshen up. Looking into a mirror she saw how pale she was. A little rouge will fix that and bright lipstick. After applying the make-up she thought, this will have to do and turned and walked out to meet Quint. What must he be thinking? Quint was relieved to see her, she looked a little better, still pale he thought.

"Where do you want to eat lunch?" he asked.

"You chose, I really don't care." He took her to the nearest Denny's and insisted she order right away. She couldn't tell him she wasn't hungry. She would try to force something down. The waitress was ready to take their order.

"I will have a cup of soup and hot tea".

"You have to have something other than that."

"That's all I want," she said.

Quint looked at the waitress.

"Give her a chicken sandwich, fries and a milk shake."

"Now be a good girl, tell the nice lady what bread and flavor of shake you want", Quint demanded. She knew she couldn't eat this food. Quint ordered the same. He held her hand and watched her intently.

"Are you really okay?" he asked with such care in his voice.

"Yes," she said and smiled.

Their food arrived, and to her it smelled awful. She tried the soup, it soothed her stomach some now she was able to relax. Quint encouraged her to try the fries and shake. She took one sip of the shake and it hit her with a wave of nausea. She ran to the bathroom, heaving in a public bathroom was not the greatest thing in the world. She heard a knock on the door.

"Are you all right?" Quint called.

"I will be out in a minute," she muttered as she heaved again. Trying to steady herself, she washed her face. Then she came out of the bathroom, she found Quint waiting on her.

"You are not okay, I am taking you to your doctor's office now."

"No," Sandy said. "I have already seen my doctor. Could you please take me home?"

"Of course I can," he said.

Chapter 22

It was very quiet on the drive to Sandy's house. Quint wanted to ask what was going on with her but he felt he didn't have the right. They had only known each other a short time, but just in a few days this woman had become a part of his life. He couldn't understand the strange attraction or bond he felt for her. Arriving at Sandy's house, he helped her out of the car and into the house. Sandy sat on the couch with her feet on the coffee table. She was feeling very weak.

"Can I get you anything?" he asked.

"Could you fix me a seven up?"

"Coming up, my lady." He entered her kitchen and started to open the cabinet to find a glass. He fixed the drink and returned to the living room and sat it on the table.

She took a sip of the drink and said, "Thank you," and smiled.

"What is wrong with you?" he asked, not really wanting to hear bad news. Sandy changed the subject.

"You told me about Shelby's obsession with having a baby, you never said how you felt." Quint looked her in the eyes.

"I wanted children just as bad as she did. I would have loved to have a son or daughter to read to at night. Be a part of their lives, watch them grow. Nothing would have been greater."

"And now?" Sandy asked.

"I suspect that time is long gone, if never."

"If you know now that you could have a child how would you feel about it?" she asked.

"Like I was on the top of the world," he said with a big smile.

"Quint, come and sit down, I have something to tell you."

He came over and sat beside her looking expectant. She hesitated, then said, "Quint, our encounter on the beach was unprotected."

"I am sorry about that," he said sheepishly.

"Well, I always used protection until that night. I am about six weeks pregnant."

"Are you saying it's mine?" Quint looked stunned.

"I always thought it was both Shelby and I that had the problem."

He thought about it for a moment, then it hit him full force; he was going to be a father. He was so happy he didn't know what to do first he was pacing back and forth across the room. Sandy had to laugh at him.

"Sandy, how are we going to handle this?" He was talking so fast. "I know we will get married."

"Wait a minute," Sandy said. "We don't even know each other."

"You like me don't you?"

"Yes, of course," she said.

"We had good sex didn't we?"

Sandy blushed and said, "Yes."

"What else is there?"

"What about love?" she asked.

"I must confess I have seen you all over town and each time I saw you, you stole a little more of my heart. My love for you is already there. I know I can make you love me in time."

She knew she already loved him too.

"Marriages have started on less and lasted a lifetime. I know in my heart we can."

Quint got down on one knee, took her hand, looked her in the eye, and said, "Sandy, will you please make me the happiness man and marry me?"

All Sandy could do was cry and kissed him.

"I'll take it that was a yes." She just shook her head yes, she could not talk.

"We have a lot of plans to make," he started. "Tell me what you want for a wedding and it's yours." He beamed.

"A simple service would be nice, nothing big," she replied.

Chapter 23

"I'll call my sister to help put things together, if that's okay with you."

"That's fine, what are you going to tell her about us?"

"Well, the truth works for me."

"Everything?" Sandy asked.

"Well not everything," he said with a wicked smile.

He took Sandy in his arms and carried her to her bed. He slowly began to undress her planting small kisses all over her body. He stopped in mid kisses and asked, "Is it okay to do this in your condition?"

"Yes, my love, it will be okay for now," she said filling with burning desire. Quint again awakened feelings in her she never thought possible. This was a man she was going to spend the rest of her life with. She knew he was what she had been looking for. Her luck had now changed for the good. Everything felt right this time, no more mistakes. Quint gently entered her body and setting her on fire.

"Please love me now," she begged.

Kissing her long and hard he filled her request to the fullest. After, they lay in each other's arms and fell asleep.

"Betty, can you and Bill come over for dinner tonight I am cooking?" Quint asked.

"What are you up to you never cook?" Betty teased.

"Come over and see," he said. "Be here at eight o'clock," and the phone went dead on her end. Betty and Bill were on time as instructed.

"Hi Sis, Bill; Bill how have you been?" Bill started to reply when Sandy entered the room carrying a tray of hors d'eourves. Quint took the tray and placed it on the table. He took her hand and introduced her to his family. Betty had a big smile on her face and a pixie twinkle in her eyes. Quint fixed them all a drink and a Seven Up for Sandy. Betty and Bill told her it was nice to meet her. Sandy felt they really meant it.

Halfway through dinner, Quint held up his glass. "I want to make a toast to the near future Mrs. Quint Jordan," he said, smiling and winked at Sandy.

Betty's mouth dropped open, then she smiled. All she ever wanted was for her brother to be happy. From the look on his face, she knew Sandy was the one to make this possible.

"How soon are we talking about?" Betty asked.

"Next weekend okay with you, Sandy?" Quint asked.

Sandy looked surprised. "Whatever you want," she said.

"Betty, will you help us?" Quint asked.

"Just try and stop me," she said.

"Sandy, we have a lot of work to do and you will have to tell me what you want," Betty blurted with excitement in her voice.

Sandy looked at Quint. "How do you feel about a ceremony on the beach at sunset?"

Quint took her hand and kissed her fingertips and said that would be perfect.

"Sandy, I will need a list of people you want to invite," Betty stated.

"I don't have any family, just a few friends," she said. Bill had been very quiet until this point, they almost forgot he was there.

"I will take care of the catering and will have the reception at our house." Betty looked at her husband with love in her eyes.

At work the next day she asked if she could see Lewis and Winnie in their office. They asked her to have a seat.

"Is something wrong?" Winnie asked.

"No, everything is good. I am getting married. I told you I don't have any family and I would like Mr. Lewis to give me away if that would be alright."

"Nothing would please me more to walk you down the aisle."

"Winnie, would you stand up with me?"

"Oh yes, dear, I would love to." Winnie looked at Lewis and giggled mentioning that this is going to be fun. Winnie hugged Sandy and kissed her cheek.

"When is the date?"

"This Sunday, on the beach at sunset," Sandy said.

"Well, young lady, you have a lot of work to do. Are you caught up on your work?" Lewis asked.

"I have a few more tickets to write."

"I want you to give them to Pat and take the week off," Lewis ordered.

"I can't do that, I haven't been here that long," she said.

"Don't you worry about a thing, you have worked very hard while you have been here. Now do as I said and go," he said not taking no for an answer.

"Winnie, could you go with me to pick out a dress?"

"Yes and I could buy mine also," she said in a happy voice.

Chapter 24

Sandy talked to Betty on the phone and she had told her she had everything under control.

"Sandy, all you have to do is show up."

"Is there something I can do for you? I have never had a sister before and I am looking forward to having you in the family," Betty told her.

"What about Shelby?"

"Well, let's just say she kept to herself. We didn't spend a lot of time with her and Quint. Shelby made it very clear she didn't want to share him with anyone. I hope you won't be that way because I love my brother and enjoy doing things with him," Betty said with tears in her eyes.

"I promise I will share, I am a people person and like having family around, since I don't have any," Sandy said.

"Well, you have family now and we are going to be close," Betty stated. When they hung up the phone, Sandy was glad Betty was taking care of everything. She was so tired these days all she wanted to do was sleep. Quint called Lewis at the travel agency and asked him to plan a great honeymoon for them. "How about Reno? The villas have private swimming pools off the bedrooms, maid service and they have their own chefs at your beck and call."

"That would be terrific, please make all the arrangements and don't tell Sandy, I want it to be a surprise," Quint said.

"Consider it done and the honeymoon is on Winnie and myself. A wedding present I know you will enjoy," Lewis said with a smile.

"I don't know how to thank you," Quint said.

"You just have to take good care of our girl," Lewis said.

"That will not be a problem, sir. Thanks again," he said and hung up the phone.

Nancy arrived as planned on Friday. She was in a festive mood.

"Sandy. I love your place, it's so cozy. Well, what do you have planned for this weekend?"

"How would you feel about a wedding?" Sandy asked.

"Sure, who is getting married?"

"I am," Sandy said. "Nancy, would you be my attendant?"

"Yes, that sounds like fun. I'll have to find a dress," Nancy said.

"We can look in the morning. Quint is taking us out to dinner. Let's get ready he will be here very soon and I can't wait for you to meet him," Nancy said.

Quint arrived at eight o'clock p.m. and Nancy couldn't take her eyes off him.

"Sandy, does he have a brother?" Nancy said with a grin.

They had an enjoyable dinner and called it an early night. Quint walked them to the door. Nancy said goodnight and went inside. Quint took Sandy in his arms and hugged her tight. He whispered softly in her ear, "This time Sunday night you will be my wife and I cannot wait."

Sandy looked at him, and murmured, "Are you sure you want to go through with this wedding?"

He said, "I have never been surer of anything in my life. I promise I will make you happy," he said and kissed her again very passionately. Sandy didn't want him to stop.

"If I don't stop now Nancy may get an eyeful or have to stay alone tonight and you go home with me". said Quint

"You had better go." He kissed her softly and turned to walk to his car.

Saturday morning Sandy awoke to the smell of bacon, eggs and coffee cooking. Nancy had made herself at home. Entering the kitchen, Nancy handed her a cup of coffee. Today, it tasted great, even the food smelled good. After breakfast, they went shopping. Nancy tried on dozens of dresses then found the perfect one with shoes to match. The beauty shop was next. There they spent three hours and had the works done. They just had enough time to go home and change before they had to be at Betty's house for dinner. Sandy was exhausted.

Arriving at Betty and Bill's they had a warm welcome with lots of hugs. Quint was waiting his turn. He took her in his arms and kissed her very passionately. He stopped when he heard everyone clapping. He blushed along with Sandy. Sandy found a chair in the corner of the room and sat down. She was fast asleep. Quint bent down and kissed her cheek and awakened her. "Dinner's ready, honey. I hope you are hungry."

"I'm starved," she said.

Sunday morning Sandy slept late, still feeling very tired. Nancy awakened her with a cup of coffee. It didn't taste so great today. Time went by fast and it was time to get ready for the ceremony. Sandy wore a white silk suit with a white pillbox hat and small veil. Nancy wore a light blue silk dress that clung to her curves. At six o'clock p.m. the limo had arrived for Sandy and Nancy. Arriving at the beach there was a red carpet for her to walk on. Betty had outdone herself. Everything was beautiful and perfect. She had a gazebo setting out on the sand, with small pals of candle lights along the carpet for the aisle. Winnie and Lewis waited for her and everyone to take their place. The wedding march began. Winnie was the first to go down the aisle, then Nancy. Lewis took Sandy's arm and patted it and gave her a loving smile.

"Here we go," he said, as they marched down the aisle. Sandy looked at Quint as he took her hand. She felt on cloud nine until a wave a nausea hit. Deep breathe, deep breathe she kept telling herself. It worked, she was able to repeat her vows pushing the nausea out of her mind. When she looked into Quint's face she knew this was right and she knew love for the first time in her life. The ceremony was beautiful and now she was Mrs. Quint Jordan.

Chapter 25

At the reception, she had to eat something before she got sick. Quint realized something was wrong and fed her quickly. She was praying please don't let me throw up today, not today please. The reception was fabulous. Betty had really worked hard. Everything turned out great. Sandy met scores of Quint's close friends. They were very pleasant and accepted her. No one seemed to have passed judgment that it had not been that long since Shelby's death. Nancy had found a single male companion. She caught Sandy's attention, smiled and winked.

Mr. Lewis went to Quint and handed him an envelope.

"Thanks, Lewis, for all your help."

"My pleasure," he said. Quint found Sandy talking to Betty. He put his arm around her and kissed her ear.

"Mrs. Jordan, are you ready to start your honeymoon."

She just smiled. "Where are we going?" she asked.

"To Rio with a villa and all that comes with it."

They arrived at the villa. Sandy was speechless. Everything was simply beautiful. The rooms were larger than anything she had ever seen. The rooms were painted a soft pale green with drapes to match.

All the windows were open with a cool breeze blowing through the whole house. Fresh tropical flowers filled the house even the bath rooms. The bath was very large also with a sunken tub for two, a separate shower and a steam room. The maid had everything perfect. The chef had prepared hors d'eurves and champagne was chilled along with Seven Up as requested. They decided to swim for a while. Sandy hadn't realized her breasts had grown so much until she put on her bathing suit. She hung out in front. She was so embarrassed but had no choice but to wear it. Quint was pleased with what he saw. The water was warm and felt great. Quint took her in his arms and said, "Mine all mine."

"I do love you," he said.

"I love you," she said. He kissed her very passionately. Her mouth was like sweet clover. She tasted his tongue with such gentleness. This was driving Quint wild. His manhood was swollen and hard. As he kissed her neck and fondled her breasts she pressed her body close to his, wrapping her legs around his waist. He lowered her suit to expose her breasts, taking one in each hand, kissing one at a time, sucking very gently. Sandy was almost incoherent with pleasure. She let her hands roam down the front of his trunks, knowing he was ready and removed his trunks. Running her hands up and down his male shaft, he let out a groan.

"Do you know what you're doing to me?"

"Yes," she said, "do you want me to stop?"

"No, no please don't stop." He picked her up out of the water and carried her to the bed. He kissed her inner thighs and her womanhood until she couldn't stand much more. She wanted him inside her. He rolled on top of her kissing her everywhere.

"This won't hurt the baby, will it?"

She just shook her head no. She was speechless. At this point he entered her very slow as before and began the rhythm which she followed until they climaxed together as one. She had never experienced anything like this before. Her whole body shook with pleasure.

"Have I died and gone to Heaven?"

"If you have, I am right there with you," he said. He rolled to his side and held her in his arms where they fell asleep.

The next two weeks were something out of a storybook. They slept late, shopped, and made mad passionate love.

Chapter 26

It ended all too soon. On their return home, for the first time, they talked about where they would live. It was decided she would move into Quint's house until he could build her a new one. Sandy felt a little funny about moving into Shelby's bedroom. She would make the best of it. When they arrived home Betty had fresh flowers everywhere. Mrs. Jones was there to greet them with open arms. She had worked for Quint fifteen years and ran their house like a tight ship. Their first night home, they had a quiet dinner. Sandy was getting the feel of the house, when the doorbell rang. It was Betty and Nancy.

"We know we should have called, but we were nosey. We want to know all the details of your honeymoon," Betty said laughing.

"Well, not all the details." They sat around and talked and laughed. Sandy remembered why Nancy was still here. She questioned Nancy as to what was going on. Nancy just smiled.

"You remember the hunk at your wedding?" "Yes," Sandy said.

"Well, he's my hunk now."

"Good for you".

"I am going to move here as soon as I can close my house in Charlotte. I even have a job thanks to you."

"Thanks to me?" Sandy replied.

"Mr. Lewis offered me one at the Travel Agency."

"That's great," Sandy said, "now we'll be working together."

Betty nudged Nancy.

"Well, I think we have taken enough of their time."

"Let's let the lovebirds have some time for themselves."

"Oh, Sandy, I hope you don't mind, I'm staying at your apartment. I will owe you rent."

"No problem, stay as long as you like." Sandy looked at Quint. "I don't think I will be needing it." They all laughed.

Chapter 27

As Sandy was getting ready for bed, she suddenly had a chill as though someone was behind her. She looked in the mirror. No one was there. She passed it off as nerves and her condition. Quint was in bed waiting for her. She slid into bed next to him and curled up in his arms. He wrapped his arms around her and held her tight. Quint kissed her ever so softly.

"Sandy, you will never know how happy you have made me. I have a beautiful wife and also a child on the way." Quint kissed her ever so softly.

Quint's passion began to set her on fire as he fondled her breasts and kissing each so softly. Sandy had never felt sexually free before. With Quint she wanted to touch and know every inch of his body. As she began to explore, she felt a vice-like grip on her hands. She jerked, realizing Quint's hands were on her breasts. Quint looked at her. "What's wrong?" "I do not know I felt like my hands were being held. It was like a cramping hurting feeling" Quint took her hands massaging and kissing each one. She turned on the bedside lamp looking at her hands She notice fresh bruising to her hands "Would you mind holding me just for tonight?

"No, but not just for tonight, but always, he said. Wrapping her in his strong arms he kissed her warm soft lips. She had never known such passion and love in her life. This is the way it is supposed to be. As they held each other that night she knew this is where she belonged

Chapter 28

At breakfast Quint said that he had to go to the office for a few hours.

"Then we will have lunch," he said.

"While you're at your office, I will pick some of my things."

"You take Mrs. Jones with you. Ask her son James to get some boxes and to carry them for you. No lifting, you hear."

"I hear you," and she laughed. "Is this the way it's going to be for the next seven months?"

"Yes," he said. He kissed her on the nose and left.

"Mrs. Jones, would your son be able to get me some boxes this morning?"

"Sure he can, I'll call him now." Sandy and Mrs. Jones left for the apartment. Nancy was just getting up when they arrived.

"I hope you don't mind my coming over but I want to move some of my things."

"Of course not, it's your apartment, I'll help you pack. I would like to take over your lease if that's okay," Nancy said.

"What about furniture, do you need some use mine?" Sandy asked.

"I could use it until I decide what to do with my things. Who would have guessed the changes of events in our lives when we met on the cruise?" Nancy said. Sandy packed the things she needed for now with the help of Mrs. Jones and returned home. Mrs. Jones helped her unpack. Mrs. Jones made lunch for them. While in the kitchen, Sandy asked about Shelby.

"Shelby was a socialite of sort. Very kind to everyone, liked charities involving children. She wanted a child so bad but would never consider adoption. No one ever knew why adoption was so upsetting to her. I feel she's still here sometimes," Mrs. Jones said.

"In what way?" Sandy asked.

"Well, let's see, sometimes if I change the way some of her favorite knickknacks are arranged, they end up the way she wanted them. I just laughed and tell her I will keep them in their place. I know there is a logical explanation for this. It's probably Mr. Quint doing it when I'm not looking."

Chapter 29

Sandy was in the bathroom applying lotion to her hands before she went to bed. As she climbed into bed she snuggled close to Quint. She began to rub his chest gently. Suddenly she felt a vice grip hold on her hands as though she was unable to move them. She cried out in pain. Quint jumped up and cried, "What is the matter?"

"I don't know. I felt like my hands were being held. It was like a cramping hurting feeling."

Quint took her hands and massaged them both, kissing each one. She turned on the bedside lamp looking at her hands. She noticed a fresh bruise on the tops of both hands. "Quint, look this wasn't there when I came to bed. I would have seen it when I put the lotion on my hands."

Quint asked, "Could you have hit them earlier and not noticed it?"

"No," she said. "The other night the same thing happened when I rubbed your chest but not as hard."

Quint laughed. "It must be Shelby. She always told me she would haunt me if I ever found another woman."

Sandy looked at him hard. "Quint, this isn't funny."

Quint realized it really wasn't funny. "I'm sorry, I don't believe in spooks."

"I don't either," she said. "This has happened twice. Mrs. Jones said she changed some of Shelby's knickknacks around and would leave the room and when she came back the knickknacks would be right back where Shelby left them before. Mrs. Jones said she would laugh and tell Shelby that she would leave them alone. Mrs. Jones thought the logical explanation was that she was moving them back when she was not looking. I'm tired, let's not talk about it anymore tonight."

"Would it upset you just to hold me tonight?"

"No, but not just for tonight, but always," he said.

Chapter 30

At dinner, Sandy approached Quint about finding a new house. He looked surprised.

"Please don't think I'm selfish but I don't feel this house isn't mine. It is all Shelby's."

"I hadn't thought about that," he said. "I'll call the Realtor on Monday and we'll put this place on the market."

"Are you sure it's okay with you?"

"I'm fine with it, whatever it takes to make you happy," he said and kissed her.

"I will not wait until Monday to call the Realtor, I will do it in the morning," Quint said.

"You don't believe in ghosts do you?" he asked. At that moment, he felt a pinch on his buttocks. He yelled.

Sandy asked, "What is the matter?"

"Ugh, Ugh, a cramp in my back. We had better stop all this ghost talk and get some sleep." They held each other tight and fell asleep.

At the office the next day Quint called and put the house on the market. Joan Wade, the realtor, said she may already have several people to show the house to. Kelly, Quint's receptionist asked why he was selling his house. Quint was reluctant to say but told her what was going on with Sandy. "I don't believe in spirits and in haunting."

"You need to talk to my psychic. She has a good reputation and has worked with the police for missing persons and checked out haunted houses," Kelly said.

"I don't think I need that," he replied.

"Think about it. What if she tries to hurt Sandy? You said she had left bruises on her hands. Let me just call her and maybe she can stop by the office this afternoon." He looked at Kelly thinking about what she had said. No one knew Sandy was pregnant around his office. "What if this is Shelby's spirit and she tries to hurt Sandy and the baby."

"Kelly, call your friend, but please keep this between us. I don't want people to think I've gone off my rocker." Kelly laughed.

"Mum's the word," she said, closing the office door behind her.

At 4 p.m. he heard a knock on the office door.

"Come in," he said. Kelly showed a tall blonde women in her mid-forties into his office.

"Mr. Jordan, I would like for you to meet Susan Bethel." Quint stood up and went around his desk to greet her. She held out her hand

"Call me Susan."

"Please call me Quint,"

"Kelly, hold all calls, please." Kelly exited the office with a smile on her face. She knew Susan could help him. Susan didn't turn Quint's hand loose right away. She noticed Quint was uncomfortable.

"Just relax. I like to get the feel of the person I will be working with." She turned his hands loose and took a seat in front of the desk. As he sat down he asked, "What has Kelly told you, about my problem?"

"She told me you thought your deceased wife was haunting your house and the bruising on your wife's hands. I know that you are working on a big trail case at this time. She laughed at the startled look on Quint's face. No I read this in the papers." Quint grinned.

"Congratulations, on the babies."

"Babies, there's only one."

"No, Quint, there are twins, a boy and a girl." He just shook his head.

"I need to go to your home as soon as possible. You can tell your wife I'm an old friend from out of town. Do you think we can do this tonight? The sooner I can get a feel of what the spirits wants, I will know how to handle it."

"That will be fine. I will let Sandy know to expect you for dinner.

Chapter 31

Will seven o'clock be all right?" Quint asked.

"Good, that will give me time to rest this afternoon. When I do this, it takes a lot out of me."

Quint and Sandy greeted Susan at the door.

"So nice to meet friends of Quint," Sandy said.

"Thank you for having me to dinner at such short notice." They entered the living room and Quint offered to make them a drinks and Sandy's usual 7-Up. "That would be great," Susan replied.

"I have some hors d'eurves in the kitchen, if you will excuse me, I'll be back." Sandy left the room. Quint looked at Susan as she began to walk around the room.

"I can feel strange energy next to you and I can feel anger coming from the energy."

Sandy entered the room with a tray of assorted cheeses, crackers and fresh vegetables. Only a few steps into the room, she almost tripped. Quint ran to her side to catch her. He looked around and there wasn't anything she could have tripped on.

Susan shot Quint a weird look. Sandy laughed with a slight blush to her cheeks. "Sandy you have a very nice home here" said Susan "This was mostly Shelby doing I haven't felt the need to change very much. She did a great job." At that point, the energy around them felt less angry. They said goodnight.

Susan said, "I hope you'll have me over again."

"Any time."

"Sandy is in danger. I can feel the angry energy around her. Sandy's episode with the steps and now the hors d'eurves may not have been due to clumsiness. I think you should tell Sandy who I am and what we suspect for her own safety."

"Okay, I will tell her tonight," Quint said.

"I suggest you go for a ride in the car. I wouldn't tell her in the house." Quint looked worried and agreed.

"Call me if you have any more problems," Susan said.

Sandy was helping Mrs. Jones finish in the kitchen when Quint came in.

"How would you like to take a walk on the beach?"

"Sounds good, let me finish here." Mrs. Jones shooed her out of the kitchen, telling her she could finish.

"We haven't been on the beach since our wedding," Sandy said looking into Quint's blue eyes.

"This will always be our special place," Quint said.

"My darling, we have to talk."

"Sounds serious."

"The woman we had dinner with tonight was not an old friend. She is a paranormal. When you mentioned about the stairs tonight my heart went to my throat. I couldn't bear for something to happen to you and our babies."

"Wait a minute. What's this about babies? I only have one."

"That's not what Susan says. It's a boy and girl."

Sandy was speechless.

"We will have to wait and see what the doctor says."

"Okay," Quint said laughing. "But this stuff with Shelby is no laughing matter. I want you to see some new houses Sunday. The sooner were are out the house the better, Sandy promise me you'll be careful. Do not be in the house alone."

"I will try not to."

"If no one is home, do not go in, promise me," Quint demanded.

"I promise," Sandy said.

Chapter 32

The next few weeks went fine, no problems. Even their lovemaking went undisturbed. Today was Sandy's first visit with Dr. Goldberg. Quint insisted on going to the appointment with her. It was 2:30 and they sat in the waiting room very nervous and holding each other's hand. Dr. Goldberg was surprised to see Quint.

"You have remarried, I see and to a very special woman. Sandy, how far along are you?"

"Two and a half months," she said.

"Well, let's examine you. Quint, you can stay or leave."

"I'll stay," he said, holding Sandy's hand lightly. Dr. Goldberg gave her a complete exam.

"Well everything looks good except your abdomen is slightly larger than most women at this stage of pregnancy." As Dr. Goldberg was checking for heart tones, a surprised look came over him. "I think I hear two heart beats but it is still a little early to be sure" he replied.

"We will make an appointment for you. Take your vitamins and if it's twins, you'll have to take it easy later in your pregnancy. Twins have a habit of coming early. Well, Quint you did well." He shook his hand and gave him a wink. Quint had a big grin on his face. Leaving the doctor's office, Quint put his arm around her.

"Well, young lady, you heard what the doctor said. You'll have to take it easy."

"Yes, boss," she said.

Chapter 33

Sunday came. They looked at ten houses, unable to decide on any.

"We will keep looking," Quint said. "I want you to have whatever you want but I want you out of that house also."

"Joan has an album of homes to look at. I'll pick out some when Joan and I meet for lunch," said Sandy.

Monday she had a full day's work ahead of her. By now, everyone in the office was aware of her condition. They fussed over her and kept telling her to take it easy. All her accounts were ready for her clients' approval. It was time to meet Joan for lunch. She told Winnie she may be late coming back.

"Go enjoy yourself," said Winnie. Joan and Sandy met at the Italian Restaurant. Sandy was glad they came to this place. All she could think about was linguini with shrimp. Joan was waiting for Sandy at the table. Sandy greeted Joan and said, "I'm starved, let's order first and we can look over the pictures of the houses while we are waiting for our food." Joan motioned for the waitress to come over.

"Are you ready to order now?" the waitress asked.

"Yes, a bowl of soup and a large iced tea." The waitress wrote down the order and left the table. Joan

Kay Holden

pulled out her photos and handed them to Sandy. There were two she liked real well.

"Joan, could we see these today?"

"Sure, I will just have to make some calls," Joan said.

"Good, I'll just go call Quint to meet us." Calling his office, she was unable to reach him. I'll just have to see them myself, she thought. Sandy was surprised she ate all of her lunch and could still walk.

Joan showed her the homes she had chosen. Sandy fell in love with the second home she saw. She could picture the nursery for the twins all decorated.

"I like this one but Quint will have the final say."

"Okay," Joan said. "We will show him when he is free."

Chapter 34

Sandy arrived home and no one was there. She had forgotten her promise not to go into the house alone. She was very tired and decided to take a nap. She hadn't been in bed very long when she felt a pillow over her face and awakened with a struggle. She was fighting for her life, when she heard the front door open. The pillow dropped and no one was there. She was gasping for air when Quint entered the bedroom. Quint went white.

"What's wrong?" She shook her head trying to calm down and tell him what had happened.

"Are you sure you didn't dream this?"

"No! I didn't dream it. I can hardly get my breath."

"Are you okay, should I call the doctor?" Quint asked trying to keep his voice worry free.

"I came home early, it was only 4.30. We don't usually get home until 5.30."

"I guess you're right." He replied. While Sandy was out of the room Quint called Susan.

I will be over shortly and bring some friends with me so we can get a read on the house.

Susan was knocking at their door shortly after the phone call. This time she brought some of her colleagues with her. They started at one end of the house and went from room to room. They could feel hostile energy around Sandy and in their bedroom. When they were finished, they all sat down to go over their findings. Susan spoke first.

"I feel there is a presence here. It is very angry. I feel it is Shelby and she is angry that you remarried and are having children. I feel she is going to do harm to Sandy and the babies. Quint, I fear for her safety. You must get her out of this house. Take only your personal items and leave the rest. The sooner, the better. Do not leave her alone again. Sandy, for your own safety and that of the babies, do not enter this house alone."

"Believe me, you won't have to tell me a second time. I will call first before coming home."

"I suggest you change bedrooms and see if this will help."

"When can we see the house you looked at today?"

"I'll call Joan and ask," Sandy said.

"Do you like the house?" Quint asked.

"Yes, very much. It has a lot of space for the babies."

"Call Joan, tell her we will take it and we want to close as soon as possible."

Joan told her the house was theirs but it would be at least 30 days before they could move in.

Sandy informed Quint of what she had said.

"This will give me time to find furniture. Can we afford all of this at once?"

"Something like that," he said. Mrs. Jones informed them dinner was ready.

"Great, I'm starved, I'm eating for 3 you know."

Chapter 35

I have to work today and get the cruise for the Johnson family finalized. They want to spend Thanksgiving on board. I pity the crew. Their sons are holy terrors. Our children will never be that way. They run all over the place touching everything and knocking them over, while their mother says, 'Boys, don't do that.' I can't get them out of the office fast enough."

"Sandy, you know you don't have to work. You can stay home and get ready for our babies"

"Thanks, Quint but I enjoy what I do, it will make the time go by faster. I will cut back to part-time if that's okay."

"With the house to be decorated and all you do whatever makes you happy, my love, but promise if it becomes too much, take an early leave."

"I will," she said, walking across the room she gave him a hug and a kiss.

"Kiss me like that again and neither one of us will get to work today." She gave him a devilish grin and said, "I will stop for now but beware when you come home tonight."

"I'll be home early," he said pinching her butt and saying goodbye.

"Mr. Jones, can you meet me at work around one o'clock? And we can start shopping for furniture?" It was early there were no customers in the office or due come in. She was hungry so she went to the cafeteria across the street a long period.

Outside the sun was shining bright and had been warm, but suddenly Sandy felt a chill and was unable to shake it off. As she entered the café, it felt like someone had pushed her. No one was around. As she started to sit down at the table, the chair fell over. Sandy became very scared and decided to sit at the counter. There's no way the stool could fall over.

"Pete, I'll have coffee with cream and a tuna on rye."

"Coming up," he said. A few minutes later Pete placed a coffee in front of her. The coffee dumped in her lap. The only reason she wasn't burned bad was the bulky clothing she had on and the cold cream she had added. Pete was so upset he gave her a towel and tried to dry her off. Sandy almost started to cry but wouldn't give in to it.

"Pete, don't worry about it. It wasn't your fault I assure you."

"But how did it happen?" Pete asked.

"I don't know," Sandy said. "Maybe you have ghosts." Pete poured another cup of coffee and held it real tight. Sandy took it from him and took a sip. Pete handed her sandwich and when she picked it up to take a bite it had a pungent order she was unable to eat it. It almost made her throw up.

"Pete, is this tuna fresh?"

"Yes, why?" he asked.

"It has a bad odor to it." Pete checked the sandwich and gagged.

"Sandy, it was okay when I fixed it this morning."

"That's okay, Pete, I wasn't very hungry anyway," she lied, she was starving. She drank her coffee and left. Outside, the cold chill was present again. This time Sandy was mad.

"What is wrong?"

"Well, Shelby made her presence known today at the coffee shop," Sandy said.

"What?!" exclaimed Mrs. Jones?

"Yes, she dumped coffee in my lap. My tuna sandwich had a pungent smell that was not there before. I am tired of her shit and she needs to stop it and she was gone."

"Are you okay?" Mrs. Jones asked. Sandy smiled.

"She's not going to slow me down. Let's start shopping."

Sandy and Mrs. Jones looked at furniture until dinnertime. This is going to take longer than she thought.

"Mrs. Jones, let's have take-out food tonight, your choice."

"Sounds good, let's have Chinese and they can deliver." When they returned home, Quint was waiting for them.

"Hi," he said, "thought you got lost."

"We did, with the time. We're having takeout tonight."

"Fine with me," he said. While they were waiting on their food, Sandy told Quint about the problem at the café. He turned pale.

"So if we move, she could still show up. Let's call Susan."

Susan listened as Sandy explained what had happened today.

"Sandy, I would like to come over and talk to you and Quint if that is okay."

"Sure, hope you like Chinese food." Susan was there before the food arrived. Sandy repeated her story as Susan listened.

"All I can suggest is try explaining how you feels and you know about her not being able to have babies but not to try and hurt yours," Susan offered.

"Do you think it will work?" Quint asked. About that time a little dog flew off the mantle and broke into a lot of little pieces. "I guess that means no," Quint said.

Susan suggested having a séance but she would have to have her friend Heather perform it because she was not gifted to communicate with the dead.

"I'll call her now and see when she can set this up."

She was able to make arrangements for the following night. "She will be bringing four other people with her to complete the circle."

Chapter 36

Friday arrived and the dining room was set up for the evening. Sandy and Quint greeted Heather and the other people at the door. There was a brother and sister that their mother had died and they could not find a copy of her will. They had hoped to get an answer to the location tonight. One man had lost his wife and couldn't say goodbye. They had been fighting when she died. The last one was a young mother who had lost a child to violence and wanted to get help as to who had killed her.

They all sat around the big table Heather giving instructions not to make sudden movements and not to be frightened. She explained the spirits would channel through her.

"Before you came tonight, I asked each of you to make a list of question. Stick to your list. There is no time limit as to how long each spirit will last" Before Heather began, she said the Lord's Prayer then asked everyone to join hands. Suddenly the room became cold, Jim and Kathy, the brother and sister mother appeared. She scolded them both for not listening to her. The will is behind the mirror in the entrance way.

The next man was Joe, he had an ugly argument with his wife just as she left the house. She was in a bad car wreck and died. He always felt if they hadn't argued she would still be here. His turn was next. "Joe, our argument didn't have anything to do with the accident. Stop blaming yourself and get on with your life. Watch out for the woman next door because she intends to marry you." She laughed and was gone.

Brenda could hear her little girl crying.

"He hurt me, Mommy. Why did he hurt me?"

"Who hurt you, darling?"

"Mike did," she said. "How did he hurt you, Wendy?"

"He took me in the car to the woods."

"Are you okay now, Wendy?"

"Yes, Mommy, I like it here but I miss you. Bye Mommy, I love you," and she was gone.

Brenda sat with tears running down her face. Mike was the man she thought she was in love with. It was killing her inside because she had let this creature into her home and he had killed her daughter. He would pay and it would not be by the justice system. He would beg for death before she was through with him.

It was Shelby's turn to be heard from.

"Why are you trying to hurt me and the babies?" Sandy asked.

Shelby said, "Those should be my babies."

"I'm sorry you couldn't have any babies but these are mine. I'm sorry you're so angry but leave me alone.

Shelby's reply was to break the mirror on the wall.

The séance was over and the other members of the group said their goodbyes. Heather stayed behind to talk with Sandy and Quint.

"What are we going to do?" asked Quint.

"Until Shelby stop's feeling as through she was cheated and cross's and to happen." Susan said.

"Didn't you say you were having twins, a boy and a girl? You might want to think about naming the girl Shelby." Sandy just looked at Quint's face.

Quint answered for Sandy. "We will think about it." They thanked Heather for coming.

As she was leaving she said, "Call me if there is anything else I can do for you." They were both quiet each in their own thought. Sandy spoke first. "What do you think about what she said about talking to Shelby?"

"Well, it couldn't hurt," Quint said.

"I like the name Shelby Lynn for our daughter." Quint just looked at her. "You don't have to do this."

"I don't have a problem with it if you don't," she said.

"Sandy, I love you so much. I think that name is beautiful. In some small way Shelby can live on through her namesake."

"Then it's settled, we just have to name our son. What do you think about Quintin Bill Jordan?"

"I like that," Quint said. "Now, all we have to do is wait for their arrival.

Chapter 37

Time was slipping by very fast, the house was ready to move into it seem there was no time for anything. Sandy was exhausted all the time now it was all she could to get up in the morning. It was moving day and the movers were here to pack their personal things. Everything else was left to the new owners. Quint had told Mrs. Jones she could have anything she wanted but she chose not to take anything. She felt it was best to leave all the old memory behind.

The new house was ready. There wasn't much to move only their personal things. It was really fun shopping for the twin's room. There were so much to choose from different styles of cribs and bed covers it was hard but she found what she wanted.

Shelby's crib was done in pink and Quinten's was all in blue. The walls had carousel horses and bright colored balloon the matching dresser. Nancy and Winnie had out done there self-there were two and three of everything. Betty said it is always good to have a pair. Everyone had brought all kind of outfits. Sandy had insisted she had to buy the outfits to bring them home in from the hospital, the others agreed but took claims on which holidays they would buy for. As Sandy stood looking at the room thinking how happy she was she felt a cold chill. Sandy knew Shelby was present.

"Well, Shelby I hope you approve." At that moment the mobile on Baby Shelby's crib moved back and forth, there were no fans or windows open.

"Shelby, let me show you all the clothes we have for the twins." Sandy took all the clothes out and placed the girls' in one pile and the boys' in the other after holding each piece for Shelby to see. Everything had to be washed before using and this was as good a time as any to get them washed. Sandy thought it sounded crazy but she enjoyed sharing with Shelby, there wasn't as much anger felt from her now.

As Sandy took a load of clothes down to the laundry the cold chill disappeared, Sandy smiled to herself. Mrs. Jones, meet her on the stairs and gave her a scolding for lifting the clothes.

"If something happens to you Mr. Quint will have my head. You go and rest now he will be home soon and I have cooked a special dinner to celebrate your new home."

"Mrs. Jones, you are too good to me," Sandy said. "I feel tired I think I will take a nap." She awoke to several voices downstairs.

Chapter 38

She entered the living room and found all the office employees and Betty and Bill everyone turned and yelled, "Surprise." Sandy was wide eyed and stunned. Quint came and put his arm around her.

Presents to open. Everything was lovely, there were more clothes for the twins and the Lewis had open a saving account for each of them.

"These children are going to be spoiled before they arrive," Quint said with a smile.

After all the presents were open Mrs. Jones announced dinner was ready. She was right that she had made a special dinner it was everything she and Quint liked. When all the guests were gone Quint and Sandy sat in front of the the fireplace with a roaring fire blazing wrapped in each other's arms.

"It was very nice for them to give us the surprise party," Sandy said.

"You couldn't ask for better friends than that," he said. "You look tired are you ready for bed?" He had a devilish look on his face as he asked. She looked at him with the same devilish grin.

"I am when you are." They giggled as they went up the stairs to their bedroom and closed the door.

Weeks went by with no visit from Shelby. Sandy felt this was a good sign. Quint came home and told her he had a client out of town that he had to represent in court.

"Can't someone go for you?"

"No, darling I have handle this client since he hired the firm five years ago. It would be impossible to try and turn over his files to someone else let alone not be fair to the client. I don't want go either but there is no getting out of it. I should only be gone three weeks or less.

"I will miss you," she said as she put her arms around his neck and kissed him. "When do you have to leave?"

"In the morning I have to catch the ten o'clock plane to West Palm Beach. I wish you could go with me. Do you think the doctor would let you travel? It could be a second honeymoon"

He kissed away her tears.

"I will be back before you have time to miss me I promise."

Sandy got up early so she could spend as much time with Quint before he had to leave for the airport. They packed his bag together. "Mrs. Jones is going to stay over until I return and you are not to be here alone. If she has to leave you call Betty or Nancy to come and stay until she returns. Make me a promise that you will do this for me."

"I will, my worry wart, we have gone over this many times when you are in town." She said, "I do love you and I will miss you very much and I would not do anything to cause any worry."

Quint kissed her long and hard then patted her on the butt.

"I had better stop or I will miss my plane." Quint gowned

"Well you could always take a later flight."

"I wish I could but my client is meeting me at the airport." He kissed her again and picked up his bag and started down the stairs with her following.

"My cab will be here in one hour so we can have breakfast together."

"I thought I was going to drive you to the airport."

"This is easier and you want to have to fight all the traffic. What are you going to do while I am gone?"

"Nancy and I are going to go through my things left at her apartment."

"Remember no heavy lifting."

"You know sometimes I think you are my mother instead of my husband. I am not a child and I am not going to do anything that will hurt our babies."

"I didn't mean it like that. I am just so afraid something will happen to you and the babies."

"I am ok, the doctor said I am doing just fine. You don't have to worry about the babies or me," Sandy tried to reassure him.

"I can't help myself. I am scared that I couldn't be so lucky to have you in my life and afraid you will disappear. He kissed her again as the cab arrived. As he gathered and everything and closed the door tears trickled down her face.

The house suddenly felt empty knowing he was gone. She joined Mrs. Jones in the kitchen for coffee.

"Well what do you have planned to do today?" Mrs. Jones asked.

"I am going over to Nancy's, she has the day off and we thought we would just hang out for the day."

Chapter 39

Arriving at her old apartment she felt like it had been years since she had lived here.

"Nancy, are you home?" she called as she entered the door.

"I am back here," she called from the bedroom. Sandy entered the room to find her sitting on the floor with boxes all around her Sandy started to laugh."

"What are you doing?"

"Well I thought since we were going to go through your things I would do the same. What we don't want we can have a yard sale."

"That sounds like fun," Sandy said. "I guess we had better get started."

They each took one of the boxes which mostly contained clothes. They each would hold up different article of clothing and laugh.

"How could we have worn some of these things?" Nancy asked.

"Well if you look at the fashion that in style now we wouldn't have to buy new clothes,"

Sandy said.

Sandy then came to the box with the family pictures and started to go through the book tears started streaming down her face. Nancy turned and looked at her.

"What is wrong?"

"These are my parents, at times like this I really miss them. Their first grandchildren, my mom would be beside herself they would be so spoiled. Mom often talked about what she would do when I had kids. It would be a job to just keep her away from them." Sandy laughed. "My parents and I were the three musketeers. We were always doing things together"

Whether it was going out to eat, vacations or just sitting at home watching TV my dad always made me feel so special." As Sandy wiped the tears away

"You are a special person and don't you ever forget it," Nancy said as she took her hand and gave her a hug.

"Thanks, I needed that. I guess I am so sentimental these days."

"I wonder why?" Nancy said rolling her eyes to focus on Sandy's belly.

Sandy just smiled. "I think I will get a larger album and put everything in order so when the babies are old enough I can tell them the story about their grandparents and tell them how much they would have loved them."

"Okay enough of this sadness, I am hungry. What sounds good to eat; we can order in or go to the beach and have hot dogs with everything on them."

"The beach sounds good. I like Steve's restaurant, he the makes his own chili and slaw I am so hungry

I know that I can eat at least three or four." Sandy laughed, then rubbed her stomach. "Eating for three gives the excuse to pig out once in a while."

At the beach the smell of surf and sand was Sandy's favorite smell of all. It reminded her of all the good times in her life around the beach. The seagulls were hungry today they were flying overhead making all kinds of racket; some people were feeding them bread; it was very pleasant to watch as they slipped down and caught the bread in midair. Inside the restaurant they took a booth so they could watch the waves break on the shore. The restaurant was just a small hole in the wall but was very clean. The chili was cooking and made Nancy's mouth water. They paced their order.

When the waitress returned with their food they went to the side bar where all the fixing were. There was so much slaw on her hot dogs you could hardly tell what was under the pile. Returning to the table they sat down. Nancy looked at Sandy and just shook her head.

"How about a walk on the beach? The wind isn't too cold, then we can have a big ice cream sundae with lots of chocolate, nuts and mounds of whip cream?" Sandy asked with a smile.

"The walk on the beach sounds good but I will pass on the sundae. You may not have to watch your waist line but I do."

Walking down the beach the warm sand felt so good between their toes, more seagulls begging for food overhead. Nancy turned to Sandy and asked, "How did you meet Quint?"

Sandy blushed and said, "On the beach."

"Okay are you going to tell me more?"

"Maybe someday but not today," she said and just kept walking, now starting to get tired.

"Well I guess we can start back for that sundae now."

As they turned to walk back Nancy was in deep thought trying to figure out why Sandy didn't want to talk about how she had met Quint. Most new brides love to talk about how they had met their husband but she would not push for now. Reaching the boardwalk Sandy kept her word and ordered the largest sundae they had with extra everything.

"How can you eat all of that? I am stuffed after one hot dog and you had two."

"I told you that I am eating for three."

"I am so glad it is you and not me," Nancy said knowing in her heart she would love to be in her place with a family on the way and have a husband like Quint. My day will come soon I hope.

At the apartment almost all the boxes had been gone through; they decided to quit for the day, as they both were tired. "Nancy, I don't think we are not going to have enough things for a yard sell. "Well what you don't want we will donate to a woman's shelter. It is so sad these women have to leave their home with only the clothes on their back. "Nancy just shocked her head

Chapter 40

A kick from her abdomen reminded her why she wasn't working. She missed working and interacting with people.

"The office is fine, why don't you come and have lunch with us tomorrow and you can visit for a while? I know everyone will be glad to see you," Nancy suggested.

"I just might do that since my days are not filled with a lot to do these days, between Mr. Jones and Quint, I am not supposed to do anything. I feel like a simple child at times the way they treat me. I know they are doing what they think is best but I am to the point I am ready to rebel."

Nancy kissed Sandy on the cheek as she left for home. After arriving home she stared to feel the effects of her lunch. As she was heaving she thought I am paying dearly now. The Tums she so flippantly remarked about didn't touch her heartburn. She finally tried warm milk and went to sleep.

She was awaked by the phone.

"Hello."

"How's my girl and our babies?"

"We are all fine. How are thing going on the case?"

"We have run into some delays and it is going to take longer that I thought. The good news is I can use my client's jet to come home on weekends if that is okay with you."

"What do you mean if it is okay with me? What time can I pick you up on Friday? I can't wait to put my arms around you. You have only been gone fourteen hours and it seems like a lifetime. I don't know how I ever got along without you in my life."

"I miss you too, darling and I don't ever want you to find out how to get along without me in your life. Well my love I have to go, everyone is ready to start the meeting. I will call you tomorrow and let you know what time to pick me up on Friday. I love you." The phone was silent. She returned the phone to the receiver, tears running down her face. Entering the bathroom she heaved again, vowing never to be so foolish again. Because it never tasted as good the second time around. Wiping her face with a cool cloth she began to feel better. After changing her clothes to remove the vomit smell she went downstairs.

Mrs. Jones was cooking dinner for them. Sandy didn't want anything to eat.

"Are you all right, Miss Sandy? You look a little green around the gills."

"I am fine, I guess what I had for lunch didn't agree with me."

"What did you have?"

"Don't ask but you can bet I won't eat it a gain while I am pregnant."

"Well try and eat a little something. I will make you a cup of special tea that my mama used to make for us kids when our stomach hurt; it will fix you up in no time." Mrs. Jones made the tea and handed it to Sandy.

"What is in this, it smells so good?"

"It has regular tea with cinnamon just a pinch, peppermint and honey. Drink all of it and I will fix another before you go to bed." Sandy sipped the tea and was halfway through with it and she realized that her indigestion was gone. She was able to eat dinner which was delicious as always. After dinner Mrs. Jones and Sandy decided to watch TV, and they both fell asleep before the first program was over. Mrs. Jones awoke first awaking Sandy to go up to bed. Up in her bed Sandy felt all alone for the first time in months. She knew that this was silly but she couldn't help it. Quint was such comfort to have him lying next to her. Friday couldn't get here fast enough.

Sandy joined Nancy for lunch at the office the next day. Everyone was glad to see her that all had to touch her stomach. Winnie took her turn and at that moment the babies decided to kick in all directions. The look on her face was priceless, she had the biggest grin on her face with tears running down her cheeks.

"Oh, Bill come and feel this, there is nothing like it."

Bill did as his wife asked, and as he touched Sandy's stomach he pulled his hand back like something had shook.

"Doesn't that hurt you when they kick that hard?"

"Sometimes it is uncomfortable but it doesn't hurt." The look on his face was that he didn't believe her; it had to hurt.

"This calls for celebration, it is not every day I get to feel my grandchildren kick their mama."

"We will turn the phones over to the service and lunch is on me." A round of applause from the employees and everyone headed to the café across the street.

Pete looked up and gave a nod of his head and smiled. Everyone placed their order and began talking at one time. The lunch went all too fast and everyone had to get back to work. Sandy felt lost because she didn't have anything to do except go and take nap.

Chapter 41

Sandy awakened to the sound of the phone ringing. "Hello."

"Hi my darling, how are you feeling?" Quint asked.

"I am fine and I miss you. I don't know what I ever did before you came into my life. You have only been gone two days and it feel like years."

"My darling I miss you too. I have some good news and some bad news, which do you want first?" he said with a little laugh.

"I guess the bad news first."

"I will have to be here longer than I first thought."

"How much longer?" The tears were running down her face now.

"About six weeks."

"Quint, I don't think I can be separated that long from you." The tears were beginning to blur her vision.

"Now the good news. My client will let me use his jet to fly home every weekend. Sandy, I love you with all my heart. I have to go now, the meeting is ready to start again. I will call again tomorrow."

"I love you too and take of yourself." She heard the phone go dead, but she felt better now. Friday I will have him in my arms and I just might not let him go, she thought as she went downstairs to tell Mrs.

Jones. She tried to find little projects she could do such as baking bread and cookies from scratch and homemade candy, which she convinced Sandy was Quint's favorite foods.

"You will have to bake a lot of cookies when those babies get here. All the school parties and such. If you lucky they want wait until the night before at bedtime to tell you. My kids did this to me I don't know how many times," Mrs. Jones said with a litter laugher in her voice and a sentimental smile on her face.

"I hope I will have the recipe down pat before they start school and then I can make then blindfolded." The house had a wonderful smell throughout. The blend of the bread baking and the cookies gave it a warm homey feeling.

"What are we going to do with all these things we have baked?"

"We can have a welcome home party on Saturday. Invite Betty and Bill and your friend Nancy, I know how much Miss Betty loves her brother. She didn't get to see him much when Miss Shelby was around," Mrs. Jones suggested.

"That sounds good, it's been a week or so since we have seen them. I will call each of them in the morning."

Friday was here and Sandy waited for Quint's call to let her know the time of his arrival.

"I don't want you to meet me, I will take a cab."

"I will pick up, my love, I don't want to wait a minute longer than I have to, to see you."

"Sandy, I don't want you out driving by yourself, it's too dangerous for you and the babies."

"Say what you really mean, all you care about is the babies and I am just extra baggage. All I have heard since we have been married is don't lift, take a nap, and take care of our babies. All of you must think I am not capable of taking care of the babies and myself. For your information I did quite well before you came along." She hung up the phone and started to cry and couldn't stop.

What was wrong with her, she thought, this wasn't like her? She would make it up to him when he got home. Upstairs she took a long shower using lustrous perfume soap that Quint liked so well. Out of the shower wrapping her hair in a towel she looked through her closet to find her panties and sexy nightgown. If I could look sexy at this point of my pregnancy, she thought, then smiled to herself. She fixed her hair just the way he liked it and put on a touch of makeup.

Looking at the clock it was nine fifteen. Heading downstairs, Mr. Jones was already in her room so she fixed a plate for Quint and placed it in the oven. Setting a place at the dining room table, she then lit a candle. Everything was in place, so, pleased with everything, she went into the living room to wait for him. She was sitting on the sofa trying to watch TV. Not able to concentrate on the program she fell asleep.

Sandy awoke with a startled feeling, looking at the TV she suddenly realized the eleven o'clock news was on. Looking around, Quint was nowhere in sight. On TV she heard the announcer say, "There was a news flash, a jet heading for Wilmington, North Carolina from West Palm, Beach Florida has crashed. There were three passengers and the pilot on board. Two are known dead and two unaccounted for. The plane burst into flames on impact. It is not known if the two missing were trapped inside or thrown clear. The names of the victims are being held until the next of kin can be notified."

Sandy gasped and began to scream.

Mrs. Jones came running. "What is wrong, are you in pain?" Sandy was shaking so hard she couldn't speak. The news announcer spoke, "A news update on the plane crash, another body has been found, still one body not accounted for. We have learned that the jet was privately owned by Morrison Company. Owner Doug Morrison is unable to be reached at present time for comment. The identity of all on board is still unknown."

Mrs. Jones was shocked, realizing why Sandy was crying. The doorbell rang and they both jumped. Mrs. Jones went to the door with Sandy behind her. When the door opened a police offer and a priest were standing there.

"Mrs. Jordan?" Sandy started shaking her head no and began to scream again.

"No, please God, not him!" then everything went black. Mrs. Jones caught her as she started to fall, gently lowering her to the floor with the men's help.

"Please call 911, she is carrying twins and this could put her in labor," Mrs. Jones asked.

Placing a cold cloth on her forehead and trying to gently awake her, there were no signs of response.

Mrs. Jones watched her breathing to make sure she was all right, then rising from the floor she hurried to the phone.

"Hello," Betty said.

"Miss Betty, you have to come to the hospital. Sandy has collapsed, the ambulance is on the way," Mrs. Jones said with trembling in her voice.

"What happened is she all right? Where is Quint?" Betty asked.

"He is not here, please meet us at the hospital and I will explain then what happened. I have to go now, the ambulance is here." Mrs. Jones returned to where she left Sandy to find the paramedics working on her.

"Can you give us some medical background on the patient?" he said as he looked at Mrs. Jones. "She is pregnant with twins and is five and a half months along. She had a shock and collapsed." replied Mrs. Jones "We are ready to transport, do you know the name of her doctor?"

"Yes, his name is Dr. Goldberg. Can I ride with you? "Yes, sit up front."

Then he got on the radio. "General, this is paramedic James. We have a twenty-eight year old female on board, unresponsive carrying twins B/P 148/90 respiratory rate 28, pulse 110. Dr. Goldberg is her doctor. Our E.T.A. is ten minutes."

Chapter 42

Arriving at the hospital work began on Sandy. Mrs. Jones was asked to wait in the waiting room. She had just sat down when Betty, Bill and Nancy entered the room. Mrs. Jones jumped up and reached out her arms to Betty, and it was at that moment she began to cry.

"Oh, Miss Betty please come and sit down, I have bad news for you."

Betty just stared at her with a blank look on her face.

"There has been a plane crash and they think Mr. Quint was on that plane. Three are known dead and one is missing, Sandy had heard it on the news, then the police were at the door then she passed out."

"You are wrong. Quint can't be dead, he has everything to live for, he is not dead," she said trying to hold back the scream in her throat.

Bill took Betty in his arms in order to give her some comfort and trying to hold back his own tears. Betty just couldn't stop shaking.

Nancy was stunned finally realizing why they were there. She went to the nurse's station and asked what was going with Sandy.

"Are you a relative?"

"Yes I am her sister," Nancy said trying to keep the fear out of her voice.

"I will have the doctor come and speak with you as soon as he is finished examining her.

Nancy returned to the others and related what she had been told and began to pace the floor. The coffee tray was brought in and the kitchen helper offered to pour for them. He could see how much stress they were under. After fixing everyone coffee he left. It had seemed liked hours since they had arrived at the hospital but had only been forty five minutes.

Dr. Goldberg entered the waiting room and asked where Quint was. Betty broke down and couldn't stop crying this time. Nancy explained what had happened.

"Well I may have some more bad news for you. Sandy has started contractions and we are giving her intravenous medication to stop the labor. If the babies are born now they don't stand a chance. It is going to be a long night. Why don't you go home and try to rest? Sandy is going to be in the Intensive Care unit and you will not be able to see her tonight. I will call as soon as I know something. Please call me as soon as you find out something about Quint. This will give me some idea how to treat Sandy, if we can stop the contractions it may be best to keep her sedated. Betty, do you want us to call your house if there are any changes?"

Bill answered, "Yes that will be fine, doctor." He put his arm around Betty and guided her to the car.

"We will all meet back at our house or you can ride with us and pick your car up later."

"Bill, I am fine to drive. Mrs. Jones can ride with me and we will meet you there," said Nancy.

Chapter 43

Eight-forty, I will be home soon and will make it up to Sandy. I guess I have been on her case about taking care of the babies. I will just have to show her how much I really love her when I get home. The plane began to hit bad weather, better use the John, before I have to put my seatbelt on. Just as he locked the bathroom door he felt the plane take a nose dive. Trying to brace his self he was forced against the wall. "Oh God please don't let me die!" he prayed. The plane plunged across the treetops tearing off the wings and a large hole in the side of the fuselage. Just before the plane crashed Quint was sucked out the whole landing on the tree branches breaking his fall. As he hit the ground a sea of blackness hit him.

Hours later he awoke to dark and cold. He didn't know where he was or what had happened. Trying to move, a sharp pain hit him and he blanked out again. When he awoke again the sun was very bright, his mouth was dry and he had cracked lips. This time he was able to move his upper body but his right left leg wouldn't move and the pain was almost unbearable. Looking at his leg he realized it was broken. A flashback of what happened, looking up to the sky, he thought thank God I am alive with tears running down his face.

No one was around, he was worrying what if no one found him.

In the distance he could hear a chainsaw and men laughing. He tried to yell but his throat was so dry. The noise stopped and he starting yelling the best he could.

Frank and Jay had stopped for lunch. Jay thought he heard something. Frank laughed at him. "You are hearing things."

"No, I swear I heard someone call for help," said Jay. "Listen, there it goes again.

"OK, I heard that. Wasn't there a plane crash in this area last night?" asked Frank.

"Let's go; look, it came from over in this direction."

Frank and Jay started calling out, "Hello!" Quint was relieved to hear them coming in his direction. He keep yelling as best he could.

Frank spotted him first, running to him. "Are you ok?"

"No, I think my leg is broken and I hurt all over."

"Jay, over here; go call for help.

Jay radioed the local sheriff's office. "We found this guy in the woods, he is hurt bad."

Jay returned to Quint; Frank was bringing him some water. That was the best tasting water he had ever had.

They could hear the siren coming their way. Frank ran to show them the way.

The paramedic was now giving him the once over and stated intravenous fluids. He was ready for transport. The hospital was three hours away so they called for airlift to meet them at the crossroads. He was sent to the hospital where Sandy was still in intensive care.

When he arrived at the ER everyone started working on him. Doctor Hess started asking questions like, "What is your name, do you know what happened?"

Quint said, "My name is Quint Jordan and I was in a plane crash." The nursed looked at the doctor and asked isn't that the last name of the lady that came in last night? The nursed called Intensive Care and asked for the name of Sandy's spouse. As the nurse suspected it was Sandy's husband. "Jill, could you have some of Mrs. Jordan's family come to ER." As Jill approached Betty and Nancy, their faces were filled with concern. "Dr. Hess would like to see you in ER."

Betty and Nancy looked at each other; one asked, "Do you know why?"

"Sorry, he just asked for you to come down there," said Jill.

As Betty and Nancy entered the ER they saw a lot of people rushing in and out of the room. Nancy stepped up to the nurse's desk and informed the nurse that they had been sent for by Doctor Hess. The nurse looked up at them and said, "Just wait here I will get him."

When Doctor Hess returned to the desk he asked who kin to Quint Jordan was.

"I am," said Betty. "I am his sister. What is wrong?" she asked dreading the answer.

"As you know he was in a plane crash, he has a broken leg, some cracked ribs and a lot of bruising."

"Will he be ok?" asked Betty with tears in her eyes and a silent prayer on her lips.

"Thank you, God. Can we see him?" Nancy asked.

"They are prepping him for surgery to set that leg."

Entering the room they were shocked to see how swollen his face was. Tears started running down Betty and Nancy's face. They walked over to his bedside and Betty took his hand and kissed it. "I thought I lost you."

He muttered through the oxygen mask and managed to say, "Not a chance."

With a weak smile he asked, "Where is Sandy?" with a puzzled look on his face.

"She isn't feeling too good, the doctors have her on bed rest but she is ok not to worry," said Nancy.

The doctor entered to room. "Ladies, I am sorry but time is up, they are ready for him in surgery."

Betty kissed his head again as they rolled him to surgery. She called, "We will be here waiting on you when you get out," trying so hard not to cry. Returning to Bill and Mrs. Jones they gave them an update, they both were so relieved to hear the news. Betty notified Sandy's nurse that they had found Quint and to please let her know that he was alive.

After several hours Doctor Hess came in to let them know Quint was going to be ok. "He will be in recovery for about an hour then he will be in intensive care for overnight. You can see him for a few minutes then."

Chapter 44

Doctor Goldberg came out and talked to Betty and the others. "Is Quint going to be ok?"

"Yes," said Betty.

"How is Sandy doing, Doc?"

"We just about have the contractions under control for now. We will start slowing down her medication in the morning and waking her up. It is still a wait and see process. I think when she knows Quint is alive that will help a lot. Why don't all of you go home and get some rest, it will be a long next few days."

"We will," said Bill, "just as soon as they bring Quint back from surgery."

Quint was still very sleepy when he returned from the recovery room. Betty kissed him on the forehead and told the nurse how to reach them.

"What a day!" Nancy said with a sigh of relief. "I don't think I will have any trouble falling asleep tonight."

"Me either," said Bill. "We will see you tomorrow, Mrs. Jones."

They all left for home with relief on their minds.

The next morning Nancy was the first to see Sandy. She was still sleeping. Nancy took her hand and Sandy slowly open her eyes. Sandy looked around the room with confusion on her face. "Where am I?"

Nancy didn't know how to start telling her what happened. "Nancy, you have to tell me what is going on?" Nancy took a deep breath; "Okay here goes." She explained that she had fainted and started contractions. "The doctor started you on some medication to stop your labor." "It is coming back to me now, oh my God what about Quint?"

Nancy looked at her with a smile on her face. "He is just fine, in fact he is here in the unit a few doors down." Sandy started to get up. "I want to see him."

The nurse entered the room at that moment. "Wait, young lady, you can't get up just yet for another 24 hours. You don't want to start labor again." "I want to see my husband." Sandy demanded. "You can later this afternoon when they get him up. He can come see you."

"Is he ok? How bad was he hurt?" she asked, trying not to cry.

"He has a broken leg and a lot of bumps and bruises but he is going to be just fine. You need your rest, please don't try to get up again until the doctor says you can." She patted her foot as she left the room. "You know she is right you need to rest. Let me get out of here so you can. I will be back later this evening to check on both of you." Nancy kissed Sandy on the forehead and left. Sandy fell back to sleep. When she woke this time Quint was at her bedside at first she thought she was dreaming. "Quint, is that really you?"

"Yes, my sweet one it is me."

"Are you ok?" she asked.

"I am fine. Are the babies fine?"

"What happened to you?" she asked.

He said, "I fell out of a plane," and laughed "Don't laugh. I thought I had lost you.

"You and those babies is what kept me alive. All I could think about was getting back to you. I love you so much I couldn't leave you."

Sandy began to cry.

Chapter 45

Sandy and Quint were both released from the hospital at the same time. Mrs. Jones had everything ready for them. The den had been turned into a bedroom. Quint wouldn't be able to go up and down the stairs for at least six weeks. Sandy was determined not to sleep alone. Quint would be lucky if she let him out of her sight.

Betty and Bill helped unload all their supplies from the hospital. When everything was in place, everyone seemed to relax. Mrs. Jones had a feast ready. Everyone enjoyed the food and everyone being together. Betty couldn't put off asking any longer as to what happened. "Quint, can you talk about what happened?"

Quint, his eyes on Sandy, began to tell what happened. "There were several times I didn't think I would not make it, then Sandy and the babies came into view and I just had to hang on." He took Sandy's hand and kissed it. She had tears in her eyes.

Bill took Betty's hand and told her it was time to leave. She agreed everyone was tired and they could use a nap. "Alone at last," Sandy said as she sat as close to Quint as she could get. His cast on his leg prevented the passionate closeness they wanted. Quint pulled her in his lap and just held her. "I don't want to ever let you go," he whispered in her hair. At that time the babies decided to kick.

"The twins may have something to say about that." They both laughed. Quint kissed her soft and tenderly and just held her.

A soft knock on the door waking them both. "Come in," Quint said.

"Sorry to wake you but your physical therapist is here."

Sandy moved, kissed Quint and got up. "Show him in."

"It's not a male," said Mrs. Jones.

Sandy looked at Quint.

In walked a young woman with blonde hair and a figure to die for. Sandy began to frown. "Hi, my name is Jenny," the woman said. "I will be working with you a few hours each day until we have you standing and in a walking cast shoe. Mrs. Jordan, please feel free to stay and watch what we are doing and you can help wherever you want. I feel the patient gets along better if family is around."

Sandy lost the jealous bug after Jenny included her. Jenny started with simple exercises just lifting the leg with the cast five times then started on the foot. Sandy was watching with such intensity that when Quint yelled with pain when his foot was flexed Sandy jumped and screamed at the same time. They all looked at each other and began to laugh.

"This is about all we are going to do today. We have to work both legs so you don't lose any muscle tone. If this same time is okay with you, I will see you tomorrow," said Jenny.

"The time is fine, it's not like I will be out and running around," Quint said.

Each day after Jenny was there except on weekends. Then Sandy and Mrs. Jones took over.

Six weeks went fast. Quint was able to walk with the support of a cane and a walking cast. In three weeks he would be back to normal except the doctors told him he would be a good weatherman after this.

He was back to work. He had been doing as much as he could on Doug Morrison's case. They had been able to postpone due to Quint's accident. He hadn't had the heart to tell Sandy he was going to have to go back to West Palm Beach Florida. He told Doug he had to get everything wrapped up in a week. Sandy was in her seventh month and it was hard for her to get around.

Sandy's doctor visits were every week now because she was carrying twins. This was about the only place she went these days. It was getting boring. The best part of her day was when Quint would come home and share his day. This made her feel she wasn't left out.

It was Friday, Mrs. Jones had fixed a roast with all the trimmings. She had planned to serve them then go and to see her son. This will give the happy couple some time alone.

After dinner Sandy and Quint curled up on the couch in each other's arms. Quint started kissing her neck and her ear which he knew drove her wild. Sandy pushed him away looked him in the eyes and remarked, "You don't play fair."

Quint said, "I know." He had a devilish grin on his face. "You know you are teasing us both don't you. Doctor Goldberg said no sex from here on out.

Sandy said with a pout, "Did he say no sex or intercourse?"

"Well intercourse I guess."

"Well, well, my love come with me and let me show you how to have sex without intercourse."

The next morning Quint told Sandy he had to go back to West Palm Beach. Sandy was not happy about this. Quint explained he would not have to travel any more after this it will only take a week.

His trip was over and he was back to his routine. He kept his days short as possible so he could spend as much time with Sandy as he could.

Chapter 46

It was early afternoon when the phone rang. It was for Mrs. Jones. It was the hospital telling her that her son had been in an accident. She so upset not knowing what to do. She was torn between leaving and staying. Quint had told her not to leave Sandy alone for any reason. Her only son needed her now. Sandy said, "Mrs. Jones, you go be with your son. I will be ok. I don't want you driving, call a cab and we will come and get you when you are ready." Mrs. Jones was grateful.

Sandy called Quint at his office but he was in court and she was unable to reach him. Nancy was at the dentist. Bill and Winnie were out. Sandy gave up trying to find someone. She had felt tired all day. As she started upstairs to lay down she got to the first landing and felt warm liquid running down her legs. Her first thought was her water broke, but when looking down she saw bright blood. Before she could take another step, she felt faint and passed out.

"911, what is your emergency!"

"My friend is pregnant with twins and has started bleeding."

"Is she conscious?" asked the operator.

"No."

"Who is calling please?"

"Shelby." "Help is on the way, cover her with a blanket." When the paramedics arrived the front door was open. The paramedics entered the room calling out, "Hello, is anyone here."

Not getting a response they started up the steps and found Sandy in a pool of blood. They gently lifted her to the first floor and placed her on a gurney. When the bleeding was checked it had slowed to a trickle. IVs were started and ER notified they were on their way. Her vital signs irregular, blood pressure was low with pulse at 120.

On arrival at the ER she was stabilized. A Pelvimetry of the abdomen showed the placenta was in the way of the birth canal. An emergency C section was needed at once. Dr. Goldberg notified surgery and neonatal I.C.U. to get ready to receive twins. "Has anyone seen her husband, if not notify him. You can get contact information from her last admission." order Dr. Goldburg

Chapter 47

The Intensive Care waiting room was across from the elevators. The door opened and Mrs. Jones looked up, her face was all red and puffy from where she had been crying. Betty and Quint rushed to her side.

"What happened to Sandy?" Quint demanded. Mrs. Jones looked puzzled. "What do you mean?"

"I am here because George was in an accident and he is Intensive Care. Is something wrong with Sandy? She was fine when I left the house. She insisted I come and she would call you."

Quint turned white and his hands were shaking. "Where is the ICU?"

"Just down the hall but they will not let you in until visiting hours which is not for another two hours."

.

Quint started down the hall with Betty right behind him. There was a buzzer which he pushed several times. The door opened with an older nurse standing there in a starched white uniform without a crease out of place. She was frowning. "My wife Sandy Jordan here?"

"Yes," she said.

"May we see her?" asked Quint.

"Not until visiting hours, she is asleep and you can't awaken her, she needs her rest."

"Where is Doctor Goldberg?" Quint demanded.

"I will have him paged for you. If I need you I will call you. You may return to the waiting room." She turned and closed the door in his face.

Quint was crushed. He was beside himself not knowing what to do.

The old battle axe has no compassion, thought Betty. "I'll fix her." Betty found a phone and called the administrator Bob Smith.

"Hi Bob, this is Betty, we have a little problem here and I was wondering if you could help us out."

"Sure, what is it?"

"My sister in law is in ICU and they want let us in to see her. My brother is out of his mind with worrying. And they won't let us in to see her. Is there any way you can help us?"

"Not a problem, let me make a phone call. Will you and Bill be at the country club dance Saturday night?"

"I hope so, depends on how things are here."

"Well, hope you can make it, we will have a lot fun. Nice talking to you, Betty. Let me make that call right now for you."

"Thanks again," said Betty.

Five minutes later the battle axe nurse greeted them with a smile saying you can see your wife now. "How nice of you," Betty said sarcastically.

Quint, Betty and Mrs. Jones followed her into the unit. The nurse started to say something about all of them coming in but though better after the phone call she just received. She just smiled and showed them Sandy's room.

She is so pale, Quint thought. The nurse who was taking care of her entered the room. "Congratulations on the twins."

Quint then realized Sandy's stomach was smaller.

"Are the twins ok?" His hands began to shake again. The nurse started to explain what happened then she saw Doctor Goldberg and stepped aside to let him take over.

"Quint, Sandy will be out for a while, she lost a lot of blood and we had to do a C-section. She's stable and she'll recover just fine; right now she needs rest. Why don't you go see your babies?"

He didn't have to tell him twice.

At the nursery window they kept looking but couldn't see them. The nursery nurse came out and asked could she help them.

"I don't see my twins," he blurted.

"Your name please?" she asked.

"Quint Jordan," he said.

"Mr. Jordan, we have them in a warmer in the back so we can keep a close eye on both of them. Each time you enter the nursery you have to put on a gown over your clothes. Next you have to use this scrub brush washing your hands up to the elbows then use this little pick for under the nails. Get a new pack each time you come in."

Quint put the gown on and did as she had instructed Betty did the same. When they were finished she led them to his babies. At first he just stood there looking at them with a big smile and tears running down his face. The nurse asked did they have names yet.

"Yes," he said. "The boy is Quint Jr. and the girl is Shelby."

Betty asked if they could hold them. The nurse smiled saying, "Sure you can. Let me take them out for you."

At first Quint was afraid to hold them. The nurse said, "Mr. Jordan, they won't break as she handed him his son. She showed him how to hold him.

Betty was all smiles. "I remember holding you like this when mom brought you home."

Quint just smiled at her. "Do you want to trade?" Betty asked.

He looked into his son's face again then took his daughter. His heart melted when he looked at her; she looked like her mother. "You just wait she will have you wrapped around her finger in no time. I have a feeling they both will."

Quint returned to Sandy's room just as she was waking up. "Oh honey, they are perfect, I just got through holding them both."

"That is not fair I haven't seen them yet," Sandy said tearfully. She pushed her call light for the nurse. When the nurse came in Sandy wanted to know when she could see her babies.

"Mrs. Jordan, let me check with the doctor and see if we can get you up," said the nurse. After a short while the nurse returned. "Doctor Goldberg said we could transfer you to postpartum as soon as a bed was ready. You will then be close to the nursery and we can get you up. It will take about an hour to move you. Then the nursery can bring you your babies."

"Thank you so much I can't wait," said Sandy. Quint took her hand and kissed it and wouldn't let her hand go.

"You have made me so happy I feel like I am about to burst." Settled in her new room, the nurse brought both babies to her giving one to each parent. Sandy held Shelby first unwrapping the blanket and counting fingers and toes. "Quint, you know what, she looks like a Shelby." They both just smiled. "You know how lucky we are they are so beautiful. Who would have thought a night on the beach would have turned out so well?" Sandy said with a wink. They exchanged babies; she did the same, unwrapped him and counted fingers and toes.

Chapter 48

Quint had to go to the office for a short time this morning but promised to be back by lunch. Around 10 a.m. the nurse brought Shelby in to be fed. Shelby latched on to the bottle like she was starving. Just as she finished feeding her and burping her a nurse came in to take the baby. A nurse she hadn't seen before. "Mrs. Jordan, I need to take the baby back to the nursery for some routine lab work."

"Do you have to take her now?"

"Yes the lab is waiting in the nursery for her," said the nurse. "I will bring her back later as soon as possible."

She leaned over Sandy and took Shelby from her arms and left the room.

A few minutes later the regular nurse Cindy came in to get the baby looking around the room she asked, "Where is the baby?"

The other nurse took her for lab work. The nurse had a puzzled look on her face. "Oh, okay I must have missed her in the hall. I will check on you in a little while. Are you ready for your son?"

"Yes I can't wait to hold him again."

"I will be right back with him."

As soon as the nurse left the room she headed to the nursery. She checked with the only other nurse

Carol, working in the nursery with her. "Did you pick up the Jordan baby girl for lab work?"

"No how could I only one nurse out of here at a time," she said. "We still have several babies to be fed in here."

They both went to each crib checking each name band making sure she hadn't been put in the wrong crib. She was nowhere to be found.

Cindy went to the floor nurse's desk and asked Liz if she had seen anyone with the Jordan baby in the hall way.

"Carol and I are the only one working in the nursery today. Neither one of us picked up the baby from Mom. Mom said another nurse took the baby for lab work, none have been ordered today."

Liz said, "Are you sure the baby is not with Mom?"

"Yes and not in the nursery."

Liz called a code brown this is the code for missing child. All doors are locked down no one in or out.

Before Liz could notify the administrator they were at her desk wanting to know what is going on. Everyone was firing questions at her all at one time, she just held up her hand for them to stop. She began to explain what had happened. "The Jordan baby girl is missing. There was a person dressed as a nurse entered Mrs. Jordan's room and took the baby saying they had to do lab work. It wasn't any of our nurses. Bob Smith the administrator took charge. Did anyone see this nurse besides the patient?" he asked.

"Not that we are aware of," stated Liz.

"How did this person get on the floor without someone seeing her?" Bob asked.

Liz looked at Bob with a sarcastic look on her face. "Do you remember all the budget cuts you made and the shortage of nurses? It is all we can do to keep up with our patients let alone notice everyone that comes on the floor. She could have been another nurse that came to visit a patient for all we knew."

"Enough! Tell Security to pull all the tapes from 9 a.m. until now and see what they show. No, just pull them and bring then to the floor. Call the police," he told Liz. "Has anyone spoken to the mother yet?"

"No," said Liz.

Chapter 49

It was noon and Quint was back as he had promised. Bending down to give her a kiss he patted her stomach, now a lot smaller. "Huh," he said with a smile. Sandy started to reply, she looked up and saw a lot of strangers entering her room. Betty entered behind them. She thought Bob was offering congratulations on the twins.

"Hello Betty, would you and Mr. Jordan have a seat?"

"Well okay," said Quint, "but is there anything wrong?"

Bob took a deep breath and began. "I hate to tell you but your little girl is missing from the nursery."

"What?" screamed Sandy, "what are you saying?"

Quint and Betty were having a hard time comprehending what he was saying. "I don't know how she could she be missing," demanded Sandy. "Where is my son?"

"He is in the nursery," said Liz.

"I want him brought me to right now," Sandy demanded as she was trying to get out of bed. As she tried to sit up on the side of the bed she became dizzied and fell back on the bed. Quint rushed to her side and helped her back in bed. "Honey, you have to stay in bed."

Bob nodded to Liz. "Bring her baby into her now please."

"What is being done to find my baby? How could this happen?"

"The police are on the way and we have the hospital on lockdown. Every room and every place a person could hide with the baby is being searched."

"Can you describe the nurse that took the baby?" Bob asked.

"I haven't seen her before. She said she had to take her for some test. She was tall with dark hair and a butterfly tattoo on her inner wrist."

Bob instructed the security guard Jeremy to pull all personnel files to see if anyone with that description worked here.

Lieutenant Janet James of Missing Persons entered the room. "Mr. and Mrs. Jordan we will do everything we can to find your child. Do you feel up working with the sketch artist?"

Junior began to cry, it was time for his feeding. Betty went to him and changed his diaper and offered him a bottle. "Betty, please let me hold him, I need to feel him close to me," Sandy said. Taking him in her arms she couldn't hold him tight enough.

"Quint, how could this happen to us she asked trying to stay calm?"

"Mrs. Jordan, I will station an officer outside your door and he will check everyone that comes in and out of your room."

As Lieutenant James left the room she spoke with Bob Smith outside of Sandy's room. "Have you heard anything from Personnel about this nurse?"

Bob called down to Personnel and talked with Jeremy to see if anyone matched this person's description.

Jeremy stated he could not find anyone with a tattoo on the wrist close to that description. "We have used a lot a temp agency nurses, check the list and call them with the description. Find out if they have anyone that they may have sent to work for us part time."

Lieutenant James entered the room with the sketch artist. "Sandy, are you sure you're up to talking with the artist?"

"I will do whatever it takes to get my daughter back," said Sandy.

"Great, he is here now, are you ready to get started? The sooner we get a description the sooner we can start looking for this woman."

Jessie West entered Sandy's room. He was very tall and very thin, dark blue eyes and a very nice smile. "Mrs. Jordan, I'm sorry for your troubles right now but I'm here to help you."

Sandy began describing the nurse who took her child. "She had long brown hair, a round face and squinty eyes; she was middle-aged."

"Okay, this starts with the shape of her face, you said it was round."

As he began to sketch he showed her the different shapes, and asked her, "Is this anything close to the shape of face?"

Sandy said, "Yes."

"Now the eyes," he said, "they were squinty, do you mean half open or just narrow slits?"

"More like half open," she said.

"What about her mouth? Did she have full lips, thin lips or in between?"

"They were not full but not thin either."

He showed her sketch of her lips. "Is this more like what you're talking about?"

"That's perfect, that's the way they looked," said Sandy.

"Now her nose."

"I remember she had a short pudgy nose."

When he was finished with the facial description he showed Sandy what he had drawn. A look of surprise came across Sandy's face.

"That's her, don't forget she had the butterfly on her inner wrist."

It only took about a half an hour to get this description drawn. Flyers were made and passed out to all hospital employees and police departments.

Sandy was beside herself. "I want to go home. I want my son at home where he will be safe and not out of my sight."

Quint tried to calm her down but he didn't have any luck. He asked Liz to call and get doctor's orders to let her go home. After an hour Liz returned to Sandy's room with orders for her to go home later that afternoon. Quint called Mrs. Jones asked her to get everything set up for them both when they arrive. He told her the FBI would be staying there for a while until Shelby could be found. "Don't worry Mr. Quint I will have everything ready, what time you think you'll be here?" she said. Getting everything ready to go home and getting the baby Quint ready, it took almost two hours before they could leave the hospital.

Chapter 50

Lieutenant James explained to them what would happen once they were home. "There will be several FBI agents setting up a block, a wiretap on the phones and following any leads that may come up. I must warn you we will be there 24/7 until we find this baby. Now is this going to be a problem for you?" she asked.

Quint said, "No, whatever it takes to find my baby."

"I am going to send ahead two of my best people to get the wiretap set and check the outlay of the house."

"That is fine," said Quint. "Let me call and let Ms. Jones know that you will be arriving before us."

Nancy and Betty came home with them to help them get everything set up and to give them more support. They brought the baby bassinet and blankets downstairs. Betty helped Mrs. Jones wash bottles and make formula. Nancy concentrated on Sandy, giving her the support she needed.

"Sandy, are you hungry, can I fix you something, and to eat you haven't eaten all day you have to keep up your strength for your son?" Nancy asked.

Sandy said, "Nancy, thank you so much but I don't think I can eat a bite."

"Okay, I will fix you some tea and maybe a few cookies, you have to eat something."

"Okay," said Sandy. Every time the phone would ring they would jump. The FBI decided that Quint would be the one to answer the phone.

The FBI would count to three before he would pick up the phone. It was when he and Lewis went to see how everyone was doing when he said, "We're hanging on, Lewis. I don't want to be rude, that we have to keep this line open."

"I understand," said Lewis, "if you need anything you can call us and we will check in with you later."

Quint was a bundle of nerves, he was pacing back and forth. Betty was watching what he was doing. "Quint, if you don't sit down you're going to wear a hole in the carpet."

She knew this was the least of his problems but it tore her up inside to see her brother go through so much pain.

Chapter 51

It had been 24 hours, no leads had shown up or calls for a ransom. Quint asked the FBI agent how long would it take for someone to call for a ransom?

The agent said, "Sometimes up to 36 hours; they want the family to really be stressed out and ready to pay any of their demands."

Sandy was so tired she just had to take a nap. Nancy promised her she would watch after Quint 'Jr'. Betty helped Sandy up to the steps and into bed. She got the baby monitor from the baby's room and set it up and took the other one downstairs because Sandy needed something so they could hear her. It didn't take Sandy long to fall asleep. In her dreams she could see herself crying and reaching out for Shelby. In her dreams she saw a street sign market and second. On this street the number 316 reappeared over and over. A woman came to the door to get the mail. It was the nurse that took Shelby! Suddenly she awoke with a knot in her throat, her face wet with tears. She got up very slowly and headed downstairs to find Quint. "I know where she is."

"What are you talking about, Sandy?"

With a big smile on her face, she said, "I know where she is."

"Who are you talking about, Sandy?" asked Quint.

"Quint, I saw the woman in the dream I just had. I saw the woman in the dream I just have the street and the house number. I even saw the woman at that address number getting her mail."

"Honey, it was just a dream, we have no proof that this is even where she said," he replied.

The FBI agents were listening as she was explaining this to Quint.

"Look, you better listen to me. I will not let my daughter stay with that woman any longer than necessary."

Lieutenant James entered the room. "What's going on?" and she started to explain about Sandy's dream.

"You have to check it out, it was so real. It was like somebody showed me where she was."

"Mrs. Jordan, I have to have more than a dream to go on," said James.

"I have a house number, can you check it out?" Sandy asked almost in tears.

Lieutenant James instructed the agent to pull up that address and see what he could find.

"Do what we have to do but do it now," Sandy said almost screaming.

"Mrs. Jordan, give me a few minutes and I'll see what I can find out. Mrs. Jordan, you have to calm down," said Lieutenant James.

"I will calm down when you find my daughter."

At 316 Second and Market Streets is a rental property. I can contact the owner of the property and see who has rented it and who was living there," stated the agent.

In just a few minutes they had the name of the people living at that address, it was a Mr. and Mrs. Callahan, the lady is within childbearing age. The property owner said that she had been pregnant but just gave birth.

"Well, Mrs. Jordan it's worth a try to check this out for you."

"How are we going to go about doing this without making her suspicious?"

"You know we can get gift bags from the hospital and go door-to-door and offer them to new mothers."

They proceeded to the address and came up with a plan to find out who on that street had just given birth to a child. They had officers and vans with blacked out windows and black SUVs. They parked at each end of the street; everything was a go. Lieutenant James and Sarah Kate decided to work as a pair. Their cover was they were offering gift baskets to all newborn mothers. The first house they chose was next door to 316. An elderly lady answered the door. They introduced themselves and explained why they were there to offer gift baskets to mothers. The lady laughed when they asked if there was an effort in her home the lady explained, laughing, and "Sam my youngest is 42 years old I don't have any infants."

Lieutenant James asked if she knew anyone on the street who might have had a baby. "Oh yes Mrs. Callahan next door just had a baby a few days ago," the lady said. "Such a pretty little girl, it is a shame her husband is overseas and wasn't here for the birth," the lady said with a sad face. "She was so looking forward for him being here."

Chapter 52

James thanked the lady and they started to take Callahan home. "Okay everyone heads up." Agent Sarah Kate instructed officers to surround the house but stay out of sight. Both Lieut. James and Sarah Kate entered the porch trying to be lighthearted with big smiles on their face. As they rang the doorbell Callahan answered the door. She was the exact description Sandy had given them. Lieutenant James explained to her that they were offering free gift baskets to new mothers. She said that her neighbor next door had told him that she just had a brand-new baby girl. "Yes, she's my little princess," said Mrs. Callahan.

"Oh she sounds precious; could we take a peek?" she asked as she offered a gift basket.

"I don't know," she said, "she's sleeping right now."

"We would love to just take a peek I promise not to wake her."

Mrs. Callahan thought for a few minutes. "Well I guess it's okay if you don't wake her up."

Both agents were wearing surveillance equipment, one that could show real time. Mrs. Callahan showed them into the baby's back room. They were able to take a picture and send it back to Quint's cell phone to see if this was their baby.

Sandy grabbed the phone from Quint's hand. Looking at the picture Sandy began to shake uncontrollably and crying at the same time. "That's my baby," Sandy screamed back into the phone.

At the confirmation of this, Agent Sarah Kate asked for a glass of water, going door-to-door to pass out these gift baskets you get awful thirsty. As Mrs. Callahan headed towards the kitchen Sarah Kate followed her. Lieutenant James picked the baby up and tried to ease out the front door. As Mrs. Callahan looked up she saw Lieutenant James with the baby.

"What are you doing with my baby?" Mrs. Callahan yelled at Lieutenant James.

"Mrs. Callahan, we don't believe that this is your baby. Until we can prove that this is your baby it has to come with us. Yes, we believe that this is a baby that was kidnapped from General Hospital two days ago."

"You people are crazy that is my baby!" she shouted.

"You have the birth certificate, the name of the doctor that delivered and the name bands that were removed when you brought her home?"

"I don't remember the doctor's name, it was a fast delivery and I didn't keep the name bands. I am telling you she is my baby and that's all you need to know," Mrs. Callahan said as she tried to take the baby from Lieutenant James.

Agent Sarah Kate gave the order for the other agents to enter the home. Callahan was crying very loudly now trying to take the baby away from Lieutenant James.

"Mrs. Callahan, you matched the description of the nurse that took this baby from the hospital. May I see your inner wrist?" And there it was, the butterfly. Other agents on the scene placed Mrs. Callahan in handcuffs and read her rights to her. Lieutenant James notified Jordan that they possibly had the baby. She instructed them to meet her at the emergency room.

"Why can't I just take my baby?" asked Sandy.

"She has to have a doctor's clearance and we also have to do a DNA on you and the baby to make sure that she is yours."

"I know she's mine," screamed Sandy.

"Well I need you both to meet us at the ER." Sandy wasn't sure she wanted to leave Quint Jr. at home. Betty and Nancy promised her that they would take good care of him.

Quint told Sandy, "Honey, you have to calm down, if this is our baby we can bring her home and this nightmare will be over."

"Don't you tell me to calm down? I will not calm down until I have her in my arms," snapped Sandy.

Sandy looked at Betty and Nancy and her son. "Are you sure you will be okay with him?"

Nancy smiled at her. "Yes, Sandy this is not the first time we've taken care of babies and we have Mrs. Jones here to help us also." Sandy started for the door and turned and looked behind her; Quint was nowhere in sight. She started calling his name. "Where are you let's go now." Betty informed her he had got the car out and was waiting on her, she almost ran to the car but was a little bit sore from surgery.

Chapter 53

At the Emergency Room the agent had already arrived with the baby and the doctor was checking her over. "Well it looks like she's taking good care of her. Her vital signs are good, she has no diaper rash and has a good set of lungs on her."

Sandy tried to go over and pick her up but until they did the DNA they could not let her have her. It took several hours to get the report back and then she was able to hold her baby. Looking into Shelby's eyes the baby looked up at her and smiled. They had been given the clearance to take her home. Sandy asked Lieutenant James, "Do we know why she took my baby?"

"Not at this time but after we cross-examine her hopefully we will find out."

When they arrived home with Shelby, the house was quiet and it seemed like this never happened. Betty and Nancy had brought down the other bassinet and now the babies were side-by-side. They all stood around and looked at them. How peaceful they were and how thankful they were that they got Shelby back. Sandy and Quint both were drained, they felt the life had just gone out of them. Betty and Nancy suggested both of them go take a nap, and that they would watch the babies until they got up. They knew how much both of them needed to rest. They took them up on their offer. Lying next to each other Quint took Sandy in his arms and held her tight. Sandy looked into Quint's eyes. "You know what I believe, your Shelby was looking out for her. How did the ambulance know to come when I started bleeding and the dream I had. If she had a hand in this I would be so eternally grateful and welcome her in our home anytime she wants to visit."

After the kidnapping things were getting back to normal. The babies were on the schedule where both of them didn't want to eat it at the same time. Sandy began to settle down and relax some. Either Nancy or Betty would come every day to lend a hand. This was the best part about being aunts. Sandy really appreciated all the help that everyone had given them and how they had been there for them.

Quint was back to work starting on a big case. He ran into Lieutenant James at the courthouse and asked if there was any update on Mrs. Callahan?

"In fact, there is, she just admitted she took Shelby because she lost her baby at seven months. She felt like if she didn't have the baby her husband would leave her. The baby was the only thing holding her marriage together. When she found out you had twins she didn't think it would hurt too much if she took one because you had another one. She will be brought up on charges of first-degree kidnapping and spend about 20 years in prison. And hopefully while she is in prison she will get some help she needs. How is everything going at home?"

"Everything is great, the babies are great. Sandy is doing great and we cannot thank you enough for all you have done for us."

Lieutenant James replied, "It was our pleasure that this turned out the way it did. A lot of times it doesn't turn out so well, you must've had divine help with this. Again I am so happy things turned out as well as they did and the best of luck to you and Sandy."

Chapter 54

Sandy had Quint install a super alarm system inside and out she wasn't taking any chances that somebody could take her babies again. Quint had cameras installed, all the windows had alarms and outside they had motion detector lights which when triggered made the yard look like daylight.

It has been five years now. The twins are growing like little weeds and they are so smart; of course, every parent thinks their child is the smartest but Sandy knows hers is. This Sunday they decided to take the twins to the beach. As they sat in the lawn chairs sipping a glass of wine they reflected back on all they had been through and how they met. Quint told Sandy, "Who would've thought that night on the beach would bring us this much happiness after all we been through. You will never know how much I love you and our twins and I'm so glad you came into my life."

"I know what you mean," replied Sandy. "You're the best thing that ever happened to me and I will love you for always."

The End

About the Author

Born in Wilmington North Carolina. Graduated New Hanover high school in 1964. Then moved to Lake Worth Florida where I attended junior college and worked as a grocery cashier. I married had a girl and a boy in Florida. Then we moved to McAllen Texas where I had another girl and another boy. I became a nurse and worked for 35 years. I retired and decided to try my skills at writing. I have written two books fiction suspense romance and the other is a children's book. I hope you enjoy them both. My writer's name is Kay Holden.

Printed in the United States
By Bookmasters